"The intimate story . . . [of a] love that
endured from teenage romance . . .
through the brink of divorce."
Newsday

THE MOMENT

Jimmy had his arms around her, his head was buried in her shoulder, and then to her amazement she felt him shuddering in her arms.

He was crying.

He was sweet and affectionate, wiping his eyes, begging her to forgive him, then crying some more. Nanci was touched beyond words. She had never seen a boy cry like this. She believed it must take a certain amount of courage for a boy to cry in front of his girlfriend. It showed that even though he might be a jock—and Jimmy liked his basketball and his hockey—he was also strong enough to show his emotions.

Holding him like this as he wept in her arms, she realized something.

She had fallen in love with him.

WITHIN A WHISPER

Also by Caroline Upcher
DOWN BY THE WATER
GRACE AND FAVOR
THE VISITORS' BOOK
FALLING FOR MR. WRONG

WITHIN A WHISPER

A True Story

CAROLINE UPCHER
with *James* and *Nanci* *LaGarenne*

HarperTorch
An Imprint of HarperCollinsPublishers

This story is based on the lives of James and Nanci LaGarenne. Certain events and names have been fictionalized to further the narrative.

❦

HARPERTORCH
An Imprint of HarperCollins*Publishers*
10 East 53rd Street
New York, New York 10022-5299

First HarperTorch paperback printing: December 2002
First William Morrow hardcover printing: September 2001

HarperCollins®, HarperTorch™, and ❦™ are trademarks of Harper-Collins Publishers Inc.

Printed in the United States of America

Visit HarperTorch on the World Wide Web at www.harpercollins.com

10 9 8 7 6 5 4 3 2 1

For Charlie Raebeck

WITHIN A
WHISPER

ONE

❦

To be a true romantic, Nanci reflected, you had to place your love for someone above everything else in your life.

She had only ever loved one man in her entire life, and his name was Jimmy. But right now, on Christmas morning, she was lying here in the spare room. For the past six months they had been living in the same house but sleeping in separate bedrooms. She had left him. Or maybe he had left her. . . .

Tonight they would share a bed again. Just for one night. For the sake of the children, because it was Christmas.

She heard him moving about in their bedroom across the landing. She heard the door open and the sound of his footsteps moving back and forth from the bedroom to the bathroom. Then they paused outside her door. She froze under the bedclothes, pulling them up over her head. Was he going to come in? How absurd to be hiding from her own husband on Christmas Day.

She heard a rustling sound, and peeping over the sheet, she saw a piece of paper sliding under the door.

It had come to this. They were communicating by notes passed under doors. She wrapped her favorite shawl around her shoulders to keep out the cold—he had brought it back for her from one of his trips to Texas—and slipped out of bed to retrieve the note.

When I've fed the animals, I'm going to get the boys up and take them out for the day. I told Harry to come around four. We'll be back by then and we can open the presents around the tree. Enjoy your day.

J.

Enjoy your day. Like he was a waiter in a restaurant who had just served her a meal. And how was she supposed to spend her day?

She would spend it, she knew, how she had spent the last six months. Brooding, thinking, going over and over what was wrong with her life. Jimmy didn't brood. That was the difference between them. He was outgoing, extroverted, full of action. And he had the ability to shut down his mind, to close it off completely from whatever problems were facing him. He was like Scarlett O'Hara. He could always think about it tomorrow.

"Mom?" Eric's head appeared round the door. Fair hair like his father's used to be, falling over his forehead . . . He wasn't her baby anymore. He was huge, almost six feet. "Mom, what's going on? Dad woke me up. Says we're going out. Are you coming?"

She shook her head, almost said, *I'm not invited.*

"Well then, I'm not going either."

"Eric," she said, in a sharper tone than she had intended, "go with your father."

"No, I'm going back to bed, I don't have to—"

"Eric, you heard me. Go with your father and—"

But he had gone.

She was worried about Eric, given the tension of the last few months, worried about both her boys but most of all about Eric. He was so sensitive, he had to have picked up on what was happening. Yet he was still a child in so many ways. He probably didn't know how to ask what was going on. The only way he could react was to refuse to join in.

Half an hour later she heard him arguing with Jimmy in the driveway, then the sound of car doors slamming, the engine being revved, and they were gone. Jimmy always managed to get people to do what he wanted. He always acted nice and in the end they always went along.

So when would he start acting nice with her, Nanci wondered, and what was it that he wanted?

She pondered all these things as she carried out her daily morning ritual, the little ceremony she performed every day before she did anything else. She lit some incense and two tall white candles. After a minute or two she burned some sage. Then she opened a gold box with an angel on top. She called it her Angel Blessing Box. If someone she cared about was sick or having a hard time, she wrote their name on a piece of paper, put it in the box, and prayed for them. For the last couple of months she had been putting two names in the box every morning, hers and Jimmy's. As she did so, she offered up her prayer: "Heal our marriage. Restore our marriage."

She ran a bath and soaked in some mint essence that was supposed to relieve tension. She washed her waist-length hair and parted it in the middle, leaving it to dry naturally, hanging down her back. Hers was always a natural look. Fresh, healthy skin, barely any makeup. Jimmy didn't like sophisticated looking women. Nanci had always been his goddess, his earth woman. She recalled her mother's despair when, instead of scouring the shops for the latest fashions, Nanci had always come running down the stairs for her dates with Jimmy in a pair of jeans and clogs.

Before her marriage, Nanci's mother had been a runway model, tall and elegant. But her daughter wasn't into glamour at all. Nanci had beautiful long dark hair and her father's flashing Italian eyes, but none of her mother's sophisticated grooming.

With the bath towel wrapped tightly around her tall, curvaceous figure, Nanci found herself wandering into the bedroom in the house she had shared with her husband for the past ten years of their twenty-two-year marriage, the room where Jimmy now slept without her. Her eye went straight to the thing she always saw when she awakened in that room: the dressmaker's dummy on which she had hung her wedding dress.

In the beginning she had had a dream of how their wedding day would be. They would get married on the beach. Their friends would sing songs they had written for the wedding; maybe someone would read a poem.

The waves, whipped up by the wind, would be pounding in the background, seagulls would fly overhead.

And she would be beautiful in a flowing white dress with flowers.

Dreams didn't cost anything and you could indulge in them anytime, anywhere. The problem was they didn't always come true. One look at her wedding dress every morning told her that. Cream, not white as she had planned, with a high bodice and long sleeves to protect her from the cold of that bitter February morning.

The bedclothes were rumpled. Jimmy hadn't bothered to make the bed. He was worse than the kids. She stripped the bed and dumped the sheets in a pile on the floor. Do the laundry on Christmas Day, why not? Besides checking the turkey in the oven, what else was there to do?

She was gathering up the sheets in her arms when her eyes came to rest on the bedside table. It had been her side of the bed in the days when she still slept there. She dropped the laundry in a heap on the floor again and sat down on the bed. She picked up a little mother-of-pearl picture frame and held it in her hands. Inside the frame, carefully mounted on old parchment paper, was a tiny gold anchor. Looking at it, Nanci almost wept. It had been one of three charms on a bracelet Jimmy had given her. Hanging from it had been three symbols, Faith, Hope and Charity. Faith was a little gold cross that she still wore around her neck; Charity had been a heart which had been lost. What did it say about her that she had lost her heart? Nanci wondered. But Hope was represented by the anchor, and she had had it framed and given it to Jimmy to put beside his bed. Then, when she had decided that he was no longer her anchor, she had moved it to her side of the bed. Slowly, she turned it over and left it lying facedown on the bedside table.

She dressed in a sweater and jeans and returned to the master bedroom. She opened an old oak chest and took out two folded white sheets smelling of lavender from the sachets she stored among her linen. And there, at the bottom of the drawer, was a bundle of letters tied up with a blue ribbon. No envelopes. These letters had never been mailed.

They were love letters, written at dawn every morning before Jimmy went to work and left on her pillow for her to find when she woke up.

She took out the top one and unfolded it. It was over a year old.

Good morning Nanci,
Thank you for a wonderful night. I love you
and always want to be with you. Your love for
me is as great as mine for you and with that we
can face anything. I'll see you later, my love,
my lover . . .

Jimmy

P.S. I fed the pigs.

Nanci almost smiled. *I fed the pigs.* With those words, you'd think she was married to a farmer instead of a cop.

She gathered up the dirty sheets and made her way down to the basement and then, as she was about to throw them in the machine, she stopped in her tracks as she always did.

She had imagined Jimmy's morning routine down here a thousand times. He rose at 4 A.M. because he had a two-hour commute and had to be at work at 6:30. He showered, shaved, and left her a note on the pillow while she lay sleeping, and then he crept silently downstairs to feed the animals.

She had no problem with Garth and Daisy, two Vietnamese potbellied pigs living a charmed life in their backyard. Every morning when she came downstairs two or three hours after Jimmy and poked her head through the screen door to see what kind of a day it was, Garth and Daisy would come snuffling toward her. *We haven't been fed. We want our breakfast, we're starving,* they seemed to be saying. "The heck you haven't," she always told them. Thanks to Jimmy's notes, she was never fooled. They were spoiled enough as it was. They had their own fenced-in area and a little wooden house where they slept. In the summer, they lounged on the deck Jimmy had built for them. The only thing they didn't have was a pool.

Knowing Jimmy, he'd probably build them one someday soon.

So she had no problem with the pigs, and she adored the rabbits, but Jimmy's menagerie down in the basement spooked her. Every time she came down to do the laundry, she had to confront them. Snakes, lizards, chameleons. They were in a special bank of illuminated glass cages he had built. You could view them through a window. Bearded dragons, frilled dragons, veiled chameleons, Bengal monitors, Savannah monitors, Sulcata tortoises, Eastern box turtles, and Madagascar hissing cockroaches. Then there was Nate the snake, a Burmese python.

That was Jimmy, he cared for all living creatures, even the ones most people found it hard to love. Even though Nanci didn't love these animals the way he did, they reminded her of what she had once loved so much in him.

And it was all she could do to stop herself from sitting down on the basement steps and weeping over the loss of what they had once had.

The hours had passed quickly. To avoid allowing the day to become one of sadness and remorse, Nanci had plunged herself into tidying up the house and fixing the best Christmas dinner they would ever have. She had made crabmeat quiche for an hors d'oeuvre. Then they would have stuffed mushrooms, turkey, mashed potatoes, and creamed spinach, Jimmy's favorite. And for dessert she had made three chocolate pudding pies because she knew the boys would want to eat it all night. Now it was already late afternoon and the family were gathered around the Christmas tree, ready to open the presents. Jason was home from college and getting ready for a trip to Australia in January. Eric, six years younger and the more athletic of the two, was already excited about the snowboard he knew he was getting.

And Jimmy had invited his brother Harry to eat Christmas dinner with them. This was typical Jimmy. He always reached out to anyone in need of help and consolation. Harry was in the middle of a divorce and Jimmy didn't want him to be on his own over the holidays. Nanci looked at Harry trying to put a brave face on things and wondered if he could possibly be feeling more lonely than she did at this point.

When Jimmy opened her present to him, she

could see he wasn't sure whether or not it was meant to be a joke. He knew how uncomfortable the lizards made her, and now she had given him a lizard calendar.

"They're your pinups," she told him as lightly as she could. "You can take it to work and hang it in your locker."

He tried to smile because the kids were watching him, but she could see he still wasn't sure.

"So," he said, pointing to a square package in Christmas wrapping hanging from one of the lower branches of the tree, "that's for you."

She waited for him to untie it and hand it to her, and when he didn't, she knelt down to retrieve it herself.

Inside was a little five-by-seven-inch wooden frame. It was pretty. Antique. Simple. Just what she liked. But now it was her turn to be confused, for inside the frame was a montage of photographs and at the top he had pasted the word *Friends*. They were little pictures that he had cut up from old photographs, pictures of her girlfriends, pictures of their mutual friends. And right at the bottom was a little picture of him. Nanci studied it. What did it mean? Was he trying to say he would always be her friend? Or that their life together as lovers was over, and now friends was all that they would be?

Then he handed her another little box.

"And I got you this."

When she opened the second present, she nearly dropped it in astonishment. It was a little green plastic alarm clock. She turned it over. The words *Made in China* stared up at her.

"It's what you need. Now you don't have to borrow mine."

The room was suddenly silent. A moment ago the boys had been ripping open their presents. Now they were shuffling uncomfortably beside the tree, looking down at the floor. Their parents were sleeping apart. Nothing had been discussed with them, but Jimmy's present had brought it out into the open.

Nanci felt the tears coming. If he had bothered to take one step inside the spare room, he would have seen that she had bought herself an alarm clock months ago. What kind of a present was it, anyway? She couldn't think of a less romantic gift than an appliance.

"I'll go check on the turkey," she said without looking at anyone and fled to the kitchen, not that she could really escape. The ground floor of their house was one big connecting circle, with the staircase rising up in the middle. You walked through the front door into the hall, turned left into the living room, which led directly into the kitchen, and on into the dining room until finally you were in the family room that led back full circle to the hall. No walls dividing any of the rooms.

In the beginning, the lack of doors had created a sense of unity within the family. Even if they were in another room, they could all hear what everyone else in the family was doing, and it was as if they were all doing it together. But in recent months, it was as if invisible walls had sprung up, separating them.

Even though she was just on the other side of the kitchen counter, and she still could see Jimmy standing by the Christmas tree, Nanci felt as if there was a closed door between them.

It was a relief to have Harry there for Christmas dinner even if she felt guilty about exposing him to their problems. Jimmy carved the turkey in the kitchen as he always did, and she piled everyone's plate high with meat, chestnut stuffing, cranberry sauce made from local cranberries. The boys and Harry cleaned their plates, but she and Jimmy barely touched theirs.

But Jimmy drank some vodka that Harry had brought along for the holiday. By the end of the meal he was feeling no pain. Nanci wondered if this would help him relax. He seemed so sad and quiet. He was making an effort for the boys and for Harry, but she could see he was just going through the motions, that he wasn't himself at all. Up to now he had been quiet, and that wasn't like him. Something was on his mind over and above the tension that had become a part of their lives.

He caught her looking at him and it was as if he could read her mind. He reached out and ruffled Eric's hair.

"Let's play Risk," he suggested.

"Yeah," yelled the boys. It was what always happened when the boys gathered round the dining room table. Any chance they got, they played a board game. With Risk you took over the world and it was all about power—male power. It was always the same when they played, their voices would get louder and louder.

Nanci stacked the dishes in the dishwasher, then went into the living room, leaving them to their game, and sat down by the fire. She listened to the sounds of raucous laughter accompanying their game and felt lonelier than ever.

She reached out to the switch on the wall and dimmed the lights in the living room. She lit a few candles instead, incense candles whose scent she hoped would calm her.

Suddenly she saw Jimmy sitting on the couch opposite her on the other side of the fireplace.

"Harry's taken the boys to see their grandmother so we could have some time to ourselves."

She had not even noticed that the game had stopped or heard the boys leave.

Jimmy had a bottle of wine in his hand and two glasses. He poured her a glass and held it out to her. His face was illuminated by the firelight. So handsome, she thought. She wondered if there was some kind of magic way they could ease their troubles and just sit here in front of the fire like lovers. No more bitter words. She took the glass from his hand.

But it was not to be.

She nearly spilled her wine when he snapped the light back on. He threw some papers down on the low table between them.

"I had my cousin the lawyer draw these up for us. Like we agreed, remember?"

She didn't say anything. He was right. She had agreed to it a while back—it was even she who had suggested they give up—but she thought he had forgotten.

"Nanci?"

Nanci fought back the tears and raised her head to look at him, dark eyes glistening.

Finally she nodded.

"Okay. Give me the papers. I need to read through them before I sign anything."

In spite of all her dreams, it had come to this. What a great Christmas it had turned out to be.

She looked at him, the only man she had ever loved and here they were.

Within a whisper of divorce.

TWO

ঙ

When you come from a family of girls, she loved to tell people, you know where there's a family of boys. Nanci DeSerio was the eldest of three sisters. Jimmy LaGarenne was number four in a lineup of six brothers. They lived right around the corner from her in Old Mill Basin. It was a typical Brooklyn blue-collar neighborhood; everybody's father was a plumber, a fireman, a policeman, or a butcher. There wasn't a lawyer on the block. The kids played stickball on the street, using the sewer plates for bases, or hung out at the candy store on the corner. The women talked over the clotheslines in the backyards and the men gathered in the front for a smoke. The streets were small enough that you could throw a ball across to your friend's house. The houses were semidetached, with two stories and shared driveways.

All around were Italians, Irish, and Germans; everybody knew everybody and everybody knew everybody's business. In this small, tight-knit community, there was no way Nanci could miss the LaGarenne brothers. Playing hockey out in the street, trick-or-treating at Halloween, they were all over the place.

She first came face to face with him when she was in the eighth grade, although she had known about him for a lot longer than that. She went around the corner to visit her friend Roseanne and saw her talking to a boy on a ten-speed bike. He had his back to her. He had dirty-blond hair. That was all Nanci noticed about him.

Then he turned around. Roseanne introduced them; Nanci took one look at his blue eyes and she was gone. They only talked for a minute, but it was enough. From then on she got a thrill in the pit of her stomach whenever she saw him.

But as it turned out, their first kiss about a month later was a disaster. They were playing

Seven Minutes in Heaven with a bunch of friends down in Roseanne's basement. It was like Spin the Bottle, only when the bottle spun toward you and him, you had to go into another room and do as much as you could get away with in seven minutes.

As they sat in a circle on the floor, Nanci willed the bottle to come to a halt in front of her. When it finally did, she reached out and spun it once again, closing her eyes and offering up a silent prayer as she did so that it would point at Jimmy sitting opposite her on the other side of the circle.

Her prayer was answered.

As she stumbled to her feet, she was so nervous her knees were almost knocking. And then, once he had led her by the hand into the darkened laundry room, she found she was shaking like a leaf as his blue eyes came closer and closer. His lips met hers; the smell of his hair was clean and sweet. She remembered wondering what shampoo he used. His arms were around her and she could tell he was a little shaky himself.

Then suddenly he pulled away.

"Don't you know you're supposed to kiss with your mouth open?"

"Uh-huh. I don't want to." This was a lie. She did want to but she knew she wasn't supposed to encourage him in any way. A strict Italian father and an old-fashioned mother had done their work on her.

"That's okay." He didn't put any pressure on her. And after his blue eyes, that was the next thing she liked about him.

They saw each other every day, always hanging out with the same crowd after school. And every now and then, he took her hand and led her off for a walk on their own.

One day after they'd been seeing each other for a couple of weeks, he asked her shyly, "Nanci, would you go steady with me?"

"Yes," she told him and waited for him to kiss her.

"So you'll open your mouth when I kiss you? I mean, now we're going steady."

But she wasn't ready for *that*!

She shook her head no. Closed her eyes and waited for him to kiss her.

Instead he snapped his fingers. She opened her eyes and looked straight into his. They were bright blue and the most beautiful eyes she had ever seen.

"What?"

"Nanci, I hate to do this but I'm breaking up with you," he said.

Just like that.

A week later she heard he had moved on to her friend Patti Doyle, who *would* kiss with her mouth open.

*L*ook, it's okay. You'll get over it," her mother tried to reason with her when she locked herself in her bedroom for days on end, filling her journal with lovesick poems.

Nanci didn't think she would ever get over it. She didn't understand. She had done the right thing, she had done what she had been brought up to do. She had been told that boys would respect her for not going too far too early. But instead of being respected, she had been dumped by the boy she knew had put a lock on her heart and claimed it as his own.

She cried until she began to wonder if she would ever stop. No matter what her mother said, it hurt! And she was not going to get over it.

"You say that now," Shirley said, "but you will, you'll see. You think it's the real thing, everyone thinks that at your age. But it isn't. It's only puppy love."

But Nanci knew her mother was wrong. Puppy love was going down to the basement with her friends and pretending to be married to the Beatles. She would be Mrs. George Harrison and her friend would be Mrs. Paul McCartney. They would make a stage out of her mother's little snack tables and stand on them and sing backup, using pencils as microphones, because that's what they imagined being married to the Beatles was like. They'd have a lot of fun, make a lot of noise, and then her mother would say the dreaded words.

"Okay, time to wrap this up. Your father will be home for his supper any minute. No more noise."

No more noise. *No more fun* was what she really meant. What did her mother know about fun anyway? Or love for that matter? All she did was clean the house, do the laundry, the marketing, and make sure her father's supper was ready on time when he came home from work. Jimmy LaGarenne wasn't a Beatle. He was real flesh and blood and she'd lost him. Her mother didn't know anything about the agony of love and loss. She'd always had Nanci's father.

At the time, she didn't realize it, but Nanci

was angry about her mother's way of life. As she was growing up, a sensitive, observant little girl, she was absorbing the atmosphere around her like a sponge. Somehow it didn't seem right to her that her father never even made his own coffee, that her mother had to do absolutely everything for him. She noticed the hurt, resigned look on her mother's face sometimes and wondered why she didn't say anything to her father. Nanci didn't quite understand how or why, but she knew she wasn't like her mother. She wasn't passive or submissive. She had her father's Italian fire inside her. If someone hurt her, she'd react, she'd do something about it.

She saw Jimmy all the time, in the street playing hockey, on a downtown bus going to school. Each time she saw him, her heart pitter-pattered and she worried that she was blushing. Sometimes she thought he gave her a quick smile when his friends weren't looking. She never smiled back, in case she was imagining it. After all, he had dumped her. But somehow a little ray of hope stayed alive inside her. Maybe one day . . .

They took the same bus although they didn't

attend the same school. Jimmy went to a public school. There was no way Mike DeSerio was going to let his daughter go to any school that wasn't Catholic. If he had his way, Nanci would be locked up in a convent for the first twenty-five years of her life. No exposure to boys whatsoever. So she was sent to a Catholic high school in a green plaid uniform with a little vest. She had to get her religious education.

She got her education, only it wasn't exactly the religious kind.

When she turned fifteen, almost three years after Jimmy had broken up with her, Nanci kissed one of the O'Connor brothers with her mouth open because she knew Jimmy La-Garenne would hear about it. Who knows, maybe something would happen. She had had plenty of crushes on other boys, but she had never forgotten that first kiss with Jimmy. And she didn't pick Sean O'Connor by accident either. She knew that if kissing anyone could get to him, it would be kissing Sean O'Connor.

Everybody in the neighborhood knew about the fight that had happened between Sean O'-Connor and Jimmy LaGarenne.

Sean O'Connor was a bully. He saw Jimmy playing baseball with his little brother Billy and he went up to Billy and told him he wanted his glove and he was going to take it.

"You're *what*?" said Billy LaGarenne, who was twelve. What did this guy want with his glove?

"I'm taking your glove and I'm keeping it." Just for the hell of it.

Jimmy went up to him. "Lay off my little brother. You're not keeping it. It's his."

And when Sean O'Connor persisted, Jimmy whacked him with his baseball bat and broke his wrist. Then he grabbed Billy and ran.

When Nanci heard about it, she was shocked. But she knew that Jimmy would be violent only when someone he loved was threatened. She knew instinctively that he was a gentle soul at heart.

The word went round the neighborhood: The O'Connors were after Jimmy. But there were only five O'Connor brothers and there were six LaGarennes, and they had Jimmy's brother Tommy. Tommy had a neck so thick it looked like his head sat on his shoulders. He played football, he went to West Point, and he was pumping iron. If the O'Connors went after Jimmy, Tommy would go after *them*.

So the O'Connors left him alone.

Secretly Nanci admired the way Jimmy stuck up for his little brother. She knew she was playing with fire when she let Sean O'Connor kiss her, but she wanted to attract Jimmy's attention. Sean was older and she didn't know if, once she got him started, she'd be able to stop him. That day, Nanci and her friends got away by the skin of their teeth. No sex—but they definitely got to kiss with their mouths open.

"We were out of there just in time," Nanci's friend Julie said when she called her the next day. "Tony O'Connor had his hand where it had no place to be."

"Did you like it?" Nanci asked, giggling.

"Too much. So listen, what are you doing after school? I'm going over to Marie Imbriale's. Want to come?"

Nanci definitely wanted to come. Marie Imbriale had a son Joe, who was Jimmy La-Garenne's best friend.

Marie made trinkets for the gumball machines. All week long she slaved away making little rings, and on Fridays the man came and took away a tower of boxes full of them. She operated from her basement. She had her TV up on the wall so she could watch her soaps, she had a little kitchen down there so she could cook, and she had her factory so she could work. Her workbench was a table with a plastic tablecloth, and all the kids from the neighborhood came over to help her. She sat the kids down on vinyl benches, gave them glue and a bunch of stones, showed them how to make rings, and pretty soon she had a regular assembly line going.

But first she fed them—spaghetti, pizza, eggplant parmigiana, delicious sauces she made up on the spot. Any kid coming through the door, didn't matter what time of day it was, they were asked the same question in a voice that had become gravelly from smoking too many Pall Malls:

"So, whaddya want to eat?"

Jimmy was hardly ever down there but there was always a chance that he might be. Joe played the drums and usually he and Jimmy would be upstairs somewhere, out of sight, having a jam session together—Joe on drums and Jimmy on guitar.

But this time when Nanci walked into Marie's basement, there he was. The noise was always at full volume—the TV going full blast in the corner, Marie shouting dirty jokes above the noise of the "factory workers" chattering away.

He looked up from the work table and their eyes met. Was he going to say anything about her and Sean O'Connor? Had he heard? Knowing the O'Connor brothers, they'd probably bragged around the whole neighborhood by now, and they'd probably said she'd done a whole lot more than kiss with her mouth open.

"So, how have you been?" They'd nodded to each other, said hi in the bus, but this was the first time in three years that they'd talked to each other.

"I've been fine. How about you?"

"Fine. So, you want to go out with me again?"

Was she hearing him correctly? All those nights she'd cried herself to sleep thinking she'd never get another chance with him, and now here he was asking her out as casually as if he were offering her a stick of gum.

She glanced at him sideways and suddenly she realized that he was nervous. He was waiting to see what she would say.

But before she could open her mouth, he said, "Don't give me your answer now. Take a while to think about it. Tomorrow is New Year's Eve. Tell me your answer in the new year. Tell me on New Year's Day."

On January first she called him to wish him a happy New Year and tell him she wanted to go out with him, but she couldn't reach him. He'd gone out with his brother Harry on New Year's Eve, drunk too much, and was spending the day in bed.

Well, this was a great start, Nanci thought. First she was embarrassed and worried. Maybe he hadn't meant it after all. But the next day, when she was about to start getting really angry, he called.

"I'm sorry I couldn't take your call. I was so sick. So, do you want to go ice skating? I want to show you how I skate backwards."

Nanci held back the words *Where have you been? I tried to get ahold of you yesterday.*

Instead she said calmly, "I don't skate. Do we have to go skating? How about we go bowling? I love that."

He laughed. "Hey, what is this? You used to be pretty shy. Now here you are kissing Sean O'Connor and telling me we're going bowling on our first date."

"Our first *new* date," Nanci corrected him. "We dated before, remember?"

"Yes," he said so quietly she almost missed it, "I remember. That's why I'm calling."

They made a date for Saturday afternoon. That was fine. She wouldn't have to explain where she was going to her parents. It wasn't as if it was Saturday night. Her grandmother was visiting from Vermont, and when Grandma Lee came, there was a family tradition for Saturday night. They all congregated in the basement, Nanci, her mother, her two little sisters, and her grandmother, where they washed and set each other's hair for church the next day. Then they would spend an hour or so dancing to Lawrence Welk. Her father would be upstairs with the ball game turned up so loud that it didn't matter how much noise they made.

And even though he made a big fuss about her getting her religious education, Nanci noticed he never accompanied them to church the next morning.

Nanci adored Grandma Lee and she looked forward to the annual summer visits to the farm in Vermont. As far as she was concerned, there had been some kind of mistake. Vermont

was where she was meant to live. She had no
business growing up in Brooklyn; she needed
the sweet fresh air of the country. The minute
they arrived, her grandma showed her how to
milk a cow and sent her to fetch the newly laid
eggs from the chicken hut and told her stories
about her mother when she was a girl.

"Grandpa Lee was so worried when he met
your father. Shirley might be a fashion model,
but underneath all that glamour she was just a
country girl. And she brought home this city
boy, this police officer. Your grandfather took
one look at him and told her to be careful. Your
father was good-looking but he was the son of
Italian immigrants from Bari on the Adriatic
Sea, and we didn't know about people like
that. We're Swedish-Irish. You get your Italian
beauty from your father, Nanci, but you get
your striking cheekbones and your height and
your carriage from your mother."

And from you, Nanci thought. *You're beautiful,
Grandma Lee.*

"Your father was from another planet. He'd
been round the world and he was hanging out
in bars in New York, places Sinatra went to. We
knew our little girl wasn't ready for anything
like that. We'd brought her up right. And to

give your father credit, he waited for her. He did the right thing by her."

Yes, thought Nanci, but look at her mother now, surrounded by all her Italian relatives with barely room to breathe, playing Susie Homemaker all day. The only way her mother had been able to survive in an Italian marriage was to be sweet and submissive. Nanci knew that would never be her way. She was aware that on the surface she appeared shy, but inside she was fiercely independent, inside she was searching for a boy—and in due course a man—who was not Italian, who would understand what a woman wanted.

She had a feeling about Jimmy LaGarenne. She'd heard it said that when you met the one for you, you knew right away. Could that really be true?

That Saturday, she put on a new pair of jeans that showed off her long legs to their best advantage. Nanci was tall for her age. Jimmy, she noticed, when she met him at the bowling alley—she didn't want him coming to the house—was still on the short side, and skinny. But the way his face lit up when he saw her coming along the sidewalk was enough to make her heart start to thump again. His face was so friendly and welcoming. He looked really pleased to see her.

But it was when he knelt down at her feet and helped her on with her shoes that she really began to tingle all over.

He looked up at her and said, "Look, I know, I was a jerk. I don't know what made me break up with you. I didn't care about Patti Doyle. I was just a kid. I'm different now. You believe that, don't you?"

Nanci nodded.

"So will you go steady with me?"

"Yes," she whispered—although in fact she wanted to shout out in joy—"yes, I will."

"So does that mean I get a kiss?"

"Later." Nanci looked around. She couldn't kiss him here, in public, in front of everyone.

"Okay," he said, "there's no hurry. I've waited three years. I can wait a bit longer."

THREE

❧

"Where's she going?" Mike DeSerio asked his wife, barely looking up from the newspaper.

Where's she going? Why can't he ever ask me directly? Nanci wondered. Why does he always have to ask my mother as if I'm not even in the room?

"She's going out for the evening," Shirley explained patiently. It was Saturday night, exactly a week after Nanci had gone bowling with Jimmy. He had told her he knew the perfect place for their follow-up date. It had better be perfect, Nanci thought. She had spent all week preparing herself for their first real kiss.

"Yes, but where and with whom? Shirley, make me a cup of coffee, will you?"

This was too much. "Why don't you make your own coffee for a change?" Nanci asked and then raced up the stairs and into the bathroom, locking the door behind her. She knew her father would be coming after her, but she was too quick for him. She waited a while and opened the door an inch.

"Leave her be, Mike," she heard her mother say. "Go see your mother. She's been asking for you."

Nanci was named after Grandma DeSerio, who was called Nunziata, the Italian version of Nanci, but sharing a name was where the similarity ended. And she couldn't really blame her father for not wanting to visit his mother. She was not a warm, demonstrative person. There were times when Nanci almost felt sorry for her father because she had never seen his mother kiss him. No wonder her father didn't know how to show his daughters he loved them.

Grandma DeSerio ruled her family with a rod of iron. She might be a woman but she was definitely the head of the family. All her sons lived either in the same house or on the same block as she did. She was the matriarch, with all her sons and their families running to and fro to do her bidding—all except Nanci's father. And he'd only escaped by running away to join the navy when he was seventeen. He was the rebel and, as he would discover, his eldest daughter had inherited his rebellious streak.

She opened her closet, trying to think what to put on. Where was Jimmy taking her? How could she dress when she didn't know where they were going? All he had said was that it would be a surprise.

But what did it matter so long as they kissed? Yet she sensed it mattered to him. Wherever it was, this was a place that would tell her a lot about Jimmy LaGarenne.

He took her to a nature reserve on the border of Brooklyn and Queens. They had to take two buses but it was worth it. It was a wildlife refuge in Jamaica Bay with a circle of walking trails, and in the middle there was a lagoon. They strolled among tall beach grass and Nanci saw that it was really a bird sanctuary. Owls and hawks eyed them as they went past, as if to say. "We know why you're here."

They came to a clearing and Jimmy led her to a stone bench.

"Out here," Jimmy told her, "I can forget I'm in Brooklyn. Out here I can pretend I'm in the jungle with loads of animals all around me. I love being with nature more than anything."

"You do?" Nanci was surprised. "I do too." And she told him all about her grandmother's farm in Vermont.

"Well, you should see my grandparents' place on Long Island," he said. "Back in the fifties my grandparents were deeded a little plot of land at a place called Lazy Point. It's on a lagoon and my grandparents built their house and it's right beside these roads of trailer parks with fancy names like Park Avenue and Madison Avenue. You walk right around the lagoon and you come to these cranberry bogs. And there's salt meadows and beach plums. My mom always takes us out of school a week before term ends and we drive out there and I take off my shoes and I'm barefoot in the sand all summer."

Of course, Nanci realized, the LaGarenne brothers were never around in the summertime. And she knew exactly what he meant by going barefoot all summer.

"Yeah, we call my mom Twinkletoes because she likes to wade out into the bay and dig the clams out with her toes. We all do, but we have to keep an eye out for the sand crabs in case we get bit. I'll never forget the day I saw my uncle standing there in the water holding up a can of beer in one hand and a bucket of clams in the other. And then slowly he began to crumple the beer can and we didn't know why. He was being bitten by a sand crab. He was in agony but all we could see was the beer can getting smaller and smaller."

Nanci laughed. She loved the way he told a story—he'd jump up and act it out as she watched.

"You know something?" he said, "That's my dream. That's where I want to wind up living some day."

This was getting interesting, Nanci thought. Jimmy LaGarenne had another side to him besides the hockey-playing jock.

"And you know what I want to do when I graduate high school?"

"Tell me," said Nanci.

"I want to drive across America in a Chevy camper van and hang out in the Rockies. I want to go for long hikes in the woods and sleep under the stars. You could come with me."

You could come with me. It sounded so romantic. She turned to look at him and found that his face was suddenly very close to hers.

"Nanci?" It wasn't really a question. He must know she wanted to by the way her lips were meeting his and her arms were going around his neck, drawing him to her. He held her very close and ran his tongue gently over her lips until she opened her mouth. It was nothing like her experience with Sean O'Connor, who had devoured her mouth as if he were taking a bite out of a hamburger. She felt the tip of Jimmy's tongue touch hers and it was the most exquisite sensation. Then it was as if her tongue were being stroked and at the same time his hand was gently smoothing the back of her head. He pulled back for just a moment, looking at her. Then he grasped her face between his hands and returned to fasten his mouth on hers with an intensity that almost scared her.

But his lips were so soft and every now and again she had a glimpse of his blue eyes.

She huddled against him, aware for the first time of the cold of the crisp January air. He removed his jacket and wrapped it around her, holding her to him.

"Thanks," he whispered in her ear, "that was worth waiting for."

They began to see each other almost every day, getting together after school to do their homework. Throughout the gloomy months of January, February, and March, he brought warmth into Nanci's life as she felt his hand clasp hers while they studied. They had to meet at Jimmy's house because Nanci didn't want him to have to face her father until it was absolutely necessary.

When she first walked into his house, she nearly died. She had never seen so many boys. His brothers just kept coming out of so many different places, up from the basement, down from the bedrooms, in from the yard. Every time a door opened, another boy walked through it. She had always known there were a lot of them, but to see them all in one house was quite something.

Jimmy introduced her.

"This is my brother Harold, he's the oldest. And this is Tommy, he goes to West Point. And here's Bobby and this is Glenn. When he was little, we used to dress him as a girl because

Mom so wanted a daughter, we felt we had to give her one."

"That's not true!" Glenn was furious.

"How do you know? How can you remember? Hey, just kidding, Glenn. And this is Billy. Billy's a champion at bumper pool."

Nanci looked at them. They all had the same turned-up nose and wide smile, but Jimmy was far and away the most handsome.

It was the noise that made the biggest impression on her. When her father was at work, the DeSerio home was a house full of girls. The atmosphere was quiet and feminine and cultivated. Her mother was a stay-at-home mom. The LaGarenne house was a whole lot rougher. Jimmy's father was a transit cop and hardly ever at home, and his mother was a nurse who worked long hours. The boys ran wild unless their father was home to catch up on his sleep, and then woe betide them if they made a sound.

"So come on down to the basement and I'll show you where I sleep."

It was like a little apartment. The four youngest brothers had to sleep down there because their grandmother had taken one of the bedrooms upstairs. There was a laundry room and the kitchen was right at the top of the stairs so they never had to go through the living room. There was even a separate entrance through the back door so if the other brothers weren't at home they could be completely private.

"Here are my gerbils," he showed her proudly, "I have a male and a female and they're gonna have babies. I used to have sea monkeys. I saw them advertised in the back of one of my comic books for a dollar so I went crazy and bought the whole deluxe kit. I dropped these little eggs into the tank and they started off the size of a dot and I trained them by shining a light on them. They were attracted to wherever I put the flashlight. I loved them."

"What happened to them?" asked Nanci. She had never met anyone who could get so excited about sea monkeys and gerbils. He had a kind of infectious enthusiasm. She had never been remotely interested in sea monkeys before, but now he had her enthralled.

"I put the tank next to my bed so I could watch them as I went to sleep, and when I reached out to shut off my alarm clock one morning, I knocked the tank over. Bye-bye sea monkeys."

"So anyway," he went on, "we can do our

homework down here and nobody's going to disturb us. My little brothers may come to take a peek at you because you're so beautiful, but I'll make sure they stay away. What are you doing tomorrow? My mom's going to drive a bunch of us to Breezy Point so we can spend the day on the beach. It'll be cold, maybe there'll be snow on the sand. But they say it's going to be a beautiful day tomorrow. We can play ball, we can play tag, we can have a whole lot of fun, maybe go to a movie afterwards. My mom will drive us there, then come and pick us up."

But of course Mike DeSerio said no way. Jimmy's mom pulled up outside Nanci's house in her big old station wagon. Nanci had seen her driving around Brooklyn so many times with all the little brothers piled in the back with their noses pressed against the window. Nanci stood at the window peeping through the curtain while her mother answered the door and explained that Nanci couldn't go. She had pleaded with her mother to get around her father, but Shirley knew it was no use.

"You know your father." It was what she always said.

Nanci gave Jimmy a quick little wave and

then turned away so he wouldn't see her crying. She wanted to rush out of the house after the station wagon, but she just wasn't bold enough, and she hated herself for it.

The next day there was a letter in her mailbox.

Dear Nanci,
I'm at the beach. I wish you were here. I'm making frozen sandcastles. Our friends are here and I feel terrible without you.

Jimmy

She wrote back to him and from that day on they wrote each other all the time. Sometimes they met and handed each other a letter to read, and sometimes they gave them to others to pass on. She would see one of the brothers in the street and hand him a letter, all sealed up, *Give this to Jimmy for me, would you, please?* And then a couple of days later, another brother would hand her a note back from Jimmy.

As winter turned to spring and spring gave way to summer, Nanci began to dread the day when Jimmy would leave for the vacation at his grandparents' house on Long Island. She wasn't sure how she was going to be able to survive the summer without him. It wouldn't be that long, but she had grown used to seeing him every day. She knew that no matter how much fun she had during summer vacation, everything she did she would imagine doing it with him. It just wouldn't be the same.

"I'll write to you," he promised. "I'll write as often as I can."

And he did. For the first time she began to receive real letters from him, arriving through the mail instead of handed to her by one of his brothers. And it was as if he were right there speaking to her. It sounded as if he wasn't having a vacation at all. He was working every day.

August 15th, 1974

Dear Nanci,
I miss you.

He always began with those words.

I am working at a motel. I am the lifeguard, the chambermaid, the towel boy, the front desk person, and the guy who does the laundry. You would be amazed if you could see me. I'm doing the whole motel. We have this woman

*here. Her name is Mimi and she gets these
headaches and she takes off so I'm left doing
everything. I work all day and then I come
back at night to show movies for the guests. I
work the projector.*

*But Nanci, here's the thing. I'm making all
these tips. I'm learning there's all kinds of people. Some people are easygoing, some are real
demanding but often they are the ones who
give the best tips. I'm making fifty bucks a
week. I keep thinking of all the things I can
buy you when I get back to Brooklyn.*

*Do you miss me too? I hope so. I sure want
to see you again soon.*

Jimmy
*P.S. Grandma called me and told me the cat ate
my gerbils!*

His letters came regularly all summer. Then
came the letter that made her heart skip a beat.
The letter itself was fine, all about how he had
threatened to go on strike unless he was paid
another twenty-five dollars a week, how he had
employed his cousin Matty to help him. Nanci
wasn't really interested. All she wanted to know
was did he miss her, did he think about her?

It was the P.S. that gave her a real shock.

P.S. I don't want to have any secrets from you so I will tell you that I kissed a girl out here last night. It was just something that happened. Nothing to worry about. She means nothing to me, not even as much as Patti Doyle. Remember Patti Doyle. Miss you a whole lot.

Jimmy
P.P.S. Her name was Jeannie but it doesn't mean anything.

Nanci agonized for days. If it didn't mean anything, why did he tell her about it? But then, she ought to be pleased that he wanted to keep no secrets from her. How could he say it was nothing to worry about? But then, he said he missed her a whole lot.

He was due back the following week. Nanci didn't write back.

The day after he returned, the first day of school, there was a letter in her mailbox.

Master James P. LaGarenne would like Miss Nanci DeSerio to help him with his math homework at five o'clock.
Dress: casual

How could she resist?

He was nervous when he let her in the door. He had grown a little and his skin was so darkly tanned, his eyes shone out like two pools of aquamarine. His hair was bleached by the sun and fell over his forehead. He held out a letter to her.

"It says I missed you like crazy and I want to kiss you," he told her.

She was in his arms in a second.

"Wow!" he said, coming up for air, "that's what I've been missing. *Ooh boy!*"

Nanci laughed, instantly forgetting all her worries. He was back in her arms and that was all that mattered.

"I spent some time with your grandmother while you were gone," she told him as they settled down to their homework. Jimmy didn't need any help with his math. He went to a special school, Brooklyn Tech. Out of the six thousand kids who took the entrance test, Jimmy had been one of the twelve hundred picked for the school.

"Oh yeah, how come?"

"Well, I missed you and I wanted to talk about you with someone."

"So what did Grandma have to say about me?"

"Not much, as it turns out. She showed me a locket and in it was a picture of your grandfather. She still wears it and I think that's so sweet."

When she had seen it, Nanci had almost cried. Maybe someday she would wear a locket with a picture of Jimmy in it. Maybe the old lady would even leave her this very locket when she died, maybe . . .

Nanci's daydreams were rudely interrupted. Jimmy was laughing at her.

"Oh boy! You've been well and truly fooled. Grandma's been telling you stories. That's not Grandpa in her locket. That's some other guy, some soldier that she loved. She didn't get to marry him. She married my grandfather and he was this big tough German guy whom she didn't even like very much in the end. My mom told me how she was always putting hairs in his soup. Hey, pass me the ruler, will you, Jeannie?"

Jeannie!

Nanci burst into tears at the slip of his tongue. She didn't really know why she was crying. She trusted Jimmy instinctively. She knew he wasn't really interested in Jeannie, whoever she was. It was just the shock of hearing him say another girl's name.

But if Nanci was upset, it was nothing to the way Jimmy reacted. She watched in amazement as he leapt up and punched his fist into the wall.

"I don't know what made me do that. I swear she doesn't mean a thing to me. You know that, Nanci, you know that, don't you? I am so mad at myself."

He had his arms around her, his head was buried in her shoulder, and then to her amazement she felt him shuddering in her arms.

He was crying.

He was sweet and affectionate, wiping his eyes, begging her to forgive him, then crying some more. Nanci was touched beyond words. She had never seen a boy cry like this. She believed it must take a certain amount of courage for a boy to cry in front of his girlfriend. It showed that even though he might be a jock— and Jimmy liked his basketball and his hockey—he was also strong enough to show his emotions.

Holding him like this as he wept in her arms, she realized something.

She had fallen in love with him.

When they parted that day, her kiss for him was extra tender and she hoped he felt everything she was trying to say with it.

The next day he handed her a note.

Nanci,
I love you more than anything. I'm sorry for before and I know it doesn't matter but I'm still sorry because I wouldn't hurt you for nothing. I don't know what I can say to express my feelings except you are the sunshine of my life and you always will be.

Love you a real lot,
Jimmy

Nanci read the note with its bad grammar and her eyes began to fill as she remembered the way he had cried in her arms and she had known beyond a doubt that she loved him. As if he could read her mind, he took the note from her hands and read it out loud to her, ending with the words she had been waiting to hear all summer.

"Nanci, I love you a real lot."

FOUR

☙

*T*hat one's got a big mouth," yelled Mike De Serio. "Why can't you do something about her?"

"My name is Nanci," Nanci yelled back from halfway up the stairs, "I'm not *that one*, I'm your daughter."

"Shirley, don't let her talk to me like that. She's not going anywhere if she talks to me like that. I'm not even going to let her out the door this summer, let alone share a house on Long Island with a bunch of people we don't even know."

"First of all, what I do outside this house is not your business—I'm eighteen and I can do what I like." Nanci had reached the top of the

stairs by now and had her hand on the bathroom door. "And second of all, if you opened
your eyes for a second, you'd know the people
I'm going with. You know my friend Lisa and
my friend Julie."

She deliberately did not add *and Jimmy*. That
would have been like waving a red rag in a
bull's face.

It was the summer of 1976, two years since
she and Jimmy had first expressed their love
for each other. Now it was as if they could not
bear to be parted from each other for more than
a day. Jimmy was preparing to go out to Long
Island for the summer as usual, and Nanci was
determined to be there for him. With two of her
girlfriends, she had the chance to rent a little
house out on Long Island, five minutes away
from Jimmy's grandparents' house. Jimmy had
a job working at the Panoramic Motel. They
could be out there for the whole summer together. They had both graduated high school
and Jimmy had saved up enough money from
the extra jobs he had been doing to buy a
souped-up kelly green Camaro that he intended to drive out to the Island. If only her father could see beyond the threat to his
daughter's precious virginity he perceived

Jimmy to be, to the hardworking, decent young man he really was.

Now that they had finally met him, her parents liked Jimmy. How could they not? Everybody liked him, because he went out of his way to be liked. And her little sisters worshipped him. For a while she and Jimmy had tried doing their homework in Nanci's basement instead of his, but her little sister Joie said she was scared of having a boy in the house, and ran and hid in the closet. And her other sister, Linda, kept running down the stairs to peek at him because he was so adorable. It was altogether too distracting.

And why couldn't her father appreciate the way Jimmy went off to work every evening after they'd finished their homework?

"You work so hard," Nanci told him, trying not to sound like a nag. *Why can't you spend more time with me? Why do you have to take on so many jobs?*

"I guess I get it from my father," Jimmy had explained. "He's a cop and he's always worked at least two full-time jobs. You see, when you're a cop they hang a carrot out. They pay you just enough to survive but not enough to live, so if you want the extra, you have to do second and third jobs. My dad always worked around the clock. I used to think he never slept. He's had all these part-time jobs for years; he just hands them on to us kids. I've got all his delivery jobs—Chinese takeout, pharmacy prescriptions, pizza."

"Well, just so long as you don't become a cop yourself," Nanci warned him.

"Me? A cop? Are you kidding? I want to be a vet, maybe a zookeeper. Anything so long as it's with animals. I'll never be a cop."

And I'll never marry one, thought Nanci.

Anyway, it wasn't even as if her virginity would be threatened if she went to Long Island and spent time with Jimmy.

Because she was no longer a virgin.

Mike DeSerio didn't know it, of course, but they'd actually been sleeping together for a year. Their first time had actually been on Long Island the previous summer.

Nanci had gone out to the Island for two weeks. Her father had allowed it because she would be staying with Jimmy's grandparents—in separate rooms. But that was at night. During the day, if Jimmy wasn't working, they had free roam of all the extensive beaches out in the Hamptons.

They went for long hikes together along a stretch of deserted beach known as Promised Land. Nanci thought it was a perfect name for such a magical place. They reached it by walking along the water's edge in front of the little fishermen's shacks at Lazy Point, stepping over mooring ropes that stretched way out into the clear blue water to a variety of rowboats, skiffs, and sailboats bobbing about in the bay. Gradually the houses petered out to a stretch of dense woodland and about half a mile of pure golden sand. They waded through the shallow water, hand in hand, chasing the sandpipers scurrying ahead of them. Jimmy was excited when they discovered the rusty remains of a ship's locker sticking out of the sand at low tide.

"Pirates!" he exclaimed.

"Buried treasure," said Nanci.

And once they had established that no one ever came near the place, they skinny-dipped. They'd never really seen each other fully naked before. There was never time to fully undress in their snatched moments of making out in the basement or the back of a car. Nanci couldn't believe how wonderful it felt to have the warm salt water caress her naked skin—until she felt Jimmy's arms come around her as she floated on her back.

"You're beautiful," Jimmy told her, pulling her along in his arms. "Holding you like this, how do I know you're not a mermaid below the waist? A siren sent here to tempt me."

"Would you love me anyway?" Nanci asked, splashing him gently.

"I'd love you more," he said, and she rolled over, ducking his head under the water until he came up spluttering for air. "It'd be like having a goldfish and a girlfriend all in one."

"Seriously," he said as they lay stretched out on the wet sand, drying themselves in the sun, "have I ever told you why I love you? It's because you're pretty, sure. But it's also because you're considerate. I get the feeling you would never consciously make someone else unhappy."

"I wouldn't," said Nanci, "unless I were so unhappy myself that I did it without thinking. That happens sometimes."

"But you're a real romantic," Jimmy persisted. "You're always doing little things to make the situation more romantic. Look at how you've put all those little candles along the ledge on my grandparents' deck. Only you would have thought of something like that."

"But it's the little romantic things *you* do that make me love you. Like the notes you write to me on the back of those cards where you record your tips for the Chinese deliveries. It shows you're thinking of me while you're delivering Chinese food."

"And how romantic is that? Actually I'm making a note that if Mr. O'Sullivan gives me a chintzy fifty-cent tip one more time, his next delivery's going to be very cold when he gets it. Only somehow it comes out as *Nanci, I love you and I can't wait for us to be together.* I wonder why."

She flicked some sand over his bare buttocks and he rolled over and grabbed her. Before she knew it, he was on top of her. *This is it,* she thought, *I'm ready.* It hurt a little as he entered her and then they were making love in the shallows like Burt Lancaster and Deborah Kerr in *From Here to Eternity.* It was slow, sensual lovemaking, warm and languid under the hot sun. As their passion increased, they created ripples spreading out from either side of them in the water, and when they were finished they lay for a long time in the wet sandy bed the pressure of their bodies had created.

"Why did we never do this before?" he whispered.

"It was never the right place or the right time. It had to be perfect. Just like when we first kissed, you took me to the wildlife reserve."

Nanci knew she was right. They kissed, they made out, they touched each other every time they met. They could have had sex any number of times, but it would have been uncomfortable, furtive, unsatisfying, and not at all romantic. This was why she loved Jimmy, because he had not rushed her into sex. He had waited until they could make love.

Those two weeks last summer had been blissful. Now they were going to have the whole summer together.

But first Nanci had to find a way to get around her father.

She felt bad about it, but the only thing to do was to involve Jimmy's mother. They told her parents that Mrs. LaGarenne was going to be out there for the summer and would keep an eye on Nanci. Of course, there was no way she would be out there for the whole summer. She was a nurse and she had to work. But Nanci's mother bought it, and she persuaded her husband that it was okay.

Nanci had also got herself a summer job on Long Island. She'd be paying her own way, so that overcame another possible objection. *Here I am, eighteen years old*, thought Nanci, *and he still treats me like I was twelve.*

She was going to be a chambermaid at another motel, one called the Albatross. Jimmy would be nearby at the motel he had aspired to working in all the summers he had been out on the Eastern End of Long Island: the Panoramic. He would have to sleep there with the other workers; the staff quarters were in the basement.

But she'd be able to spend a lot of time with him there.

On the drive out from the city, Nanci tried to picture their little love nest, but when they finally arrived, hot and exhausted, and saw where Jimmy would be sleeping, all she could do was shudder. It was a pretty miserable place, with a linoleum floor and a drain in the middle, a kitchen with a dirty sink. It was right in the pits of the hotel, but there was an upside. It was the closest possible location to the ocean.

When she spent nights there with him, she soon discovered that if you left the window open at night, you could go to sleep to the sound of the ocean. And in the morning you could open the door, run across the sand, and plunge straight into the waves. It was a wonderful experience to be able to lie in Jimmy's arms and listen to the pounding of his heart in his chest marking time with the pounding of the ocean outside.

But Nanci's favorite place was her little cottage, because it was right on the edge of Promised Land. The bay was at the end of the road, she and Jimmy would be together for the whole summer, and her parents were a hundred miles away. Her friends Lisa and Julie were already at the cottage and had made it pretty and welcoming with flowers in the bedrooms and plenty of food in the refrigerator. But all three girls knew the score. They wouldn't be seeing much of each other that summer. Lisa and Julie both had boyfriends working in the area, and Nanci had Jimmy. Nanci thought it would be surprising if they were ever all there at once for the night. In a way, she was sad that she would not be spending more time with them. But then again, one of her dreams had come true. She was independent at last.

Nanci had read about the Summer of Love. Now, in 1976, nearly ten years after the real one, she was determined to experience her own Summer of Love. Was she the only girl in America who was still arguing with her father to be allowed to spread her wings? Was it because she was the daughter of a cop?

But although she came out to Long Island thinking she had an open mind, ready for anything, Nanci was not prepared for the people she would encounter. Her first shock came when a couple in their sixties, instead of leaving her a tip at the motel, presented her with some pot to smoke.

Then, on a walk down to the bay, she met Lola.

And when she met her, Lola didn't have a stitch of clothing on.

Nanci looked away. She had never seen a naked woman outside before.

"Hi, honey," said Lola, "what's your name?" She was voluptuous and blonde.

Nanci said her name and looked away.

"Oh, are you a shy girl? Come join us, take your clothes off, let the sun warm your skin."

Nanci was tempted. She could recall how the sun had warmed her skin that day at Promised Land when she and Jimmy had first made love. But it didn't feel right to take her clothes off in front of this total stranger.

"You live around here?" Lola asked.

"I'm renting a little cottage for the summer, up the road there."

"Oh, you are? We're renting this house here. People come and go. We're an open house."

Nanci could see that virtually everyone in the backyard was wandering around naked. All the women had very long hair. Quite a few of the men too. A quick glance told Nanci they were older than she.

"Come eat with us," said Lola and before she knew what was happening, Nanci was sitting at a long table eating a mess of bean sprouts out of a wooden bowl. There was something very easy and open about these people; you found yourself drawn in before you even realized it.

"Where are you all from?" she asked politely.

"All over," said one man.

"Does it matter?" said another.

"Mickey and I have lived in Florida. Before that I was in Canada," Lola said.

"Is Lola your wife?" Nanci asked Mickey.

"No, she's mine," said another man, "but I loan her out whenever he wants her."

"You know, you're very beautiful," Mickey told her, moving closer to her on the bench.

"Isn't she just?" commented the man sitting next to her.

"My boyfriend works at the Panoramic," Nanci said quickly.

"So?" Mickey said, "What's that got to do with anything? I do too. What's his name? He probably works for me. I'm one of the managers."

"Leave her alone," Lola said, laughing. "We're all working at the Panoramic for the summer, Nanci. . . . Maybe I'll see your boyfriend. Is he cute?"

"He's my boyfriend," Nanci repeated, feeling foolish and uncomfortable. She didn't understand these people sitting there naked or partially clothed, seemingly without a care in the world.

But later on, with Jimmy beside her when

they visited Merrill's at the end of her road, a bar and pool hall right on the water, she relaxed. She had thought she was so free and independent, but somehow she needed Jimmy by her side to show these people who she really was. They loved Jimmy—as everyone did—and drew him into their circle. Soon they were all drinking together every night, playing the guitar, singing, playing pool. Nanci learned how to grow bean sprouts from Lola in the little yard behind her cottage.

"You know, Mickey's really attracted to you," Lola said one day as they were lying on an old mattress they had pulled out onto Lola's deck. "He'd like to get together with you."

"I'm with Jimmy,"

"Yeah, we know, but wouldn't you like to try a new brand to see what it's like?"

Nanci was shocked.

"I love Jimmy. I could never do that."

"Sure you do. And sure you could," Lola said, "when you're ready. Think about it."

"I'll think about it," Nanci promised. But only to get Lola off the subject. There was no way she was going to do anything. She understood now that she and Jimmy had been living in their own little insular environment in Brooklyn. They hadn't needed other people and maybe they had allowed themselves to become a little cut off. She liked Lola, in fact she and Jimmy enjoyed hanging out with all of them, but that didn't mean she wanted to sleep with any of them. She had Jimmy. She didn't need anyone else.

One night she was sitting in the cottage, waiting for Jimmy to call and say he was through working for the day. This had become their routine almost every evening; they'd each finish work and talk on the phone to make a plan for the evening. Sometimes Jimmy had to work late but he always called to tell her so.

But as the hours went by with no call, Nanci grew restless. Lisa and Julie had already left to go out for the evening, and she was all alone. Then she heard a car draw up outside and she rushed to the screen door, but it was Ricky, Jimmy's cousin.

"Ricky, take me over to the Panoramic so I can wait for Jimmy to get off work,"

It was late. Ricky wasn't so keen. "Oh, I

don't know. You don't really want to go there at this hour."

"Oh, I absolutely do," Nanci said, "Right now."

She never knew what it was that made her insist on going. She could see Ricky was reluctant, but it only made her more determined, and she had a feeling that something was drawing her to Jimmy. Ricky waited in the car while she went down the steps of the hotel to the basement and knocked on Jimmy's door. If he had finished work, he'd be down there.

No answer.

Ricky got out of the car and started pacing up and down.

"Look, no one's answering. Let's go."

Why was Ricky so jumpy? Nanci wondered.

"There's a light. Somebody *is* there."

"Okay, well, I'll leave you here." And Ricky took off without another word.

Nanci banged on the door again.

Suddenly it opened and Jimmy stood there. She moved toward him, expecting him to put his arms around her and kiss her as he normally did, but to her surprise he backed away.

She tried to push the door open.

"What's up? Were you asleep? Let me in."

"What are you doing here? What do you want?"

Nanci reeled. He had never spoken to her like this before. There was no warmth in his tone. Worse, there was no love.

She walked past him into his bedroom and stopped dead. Somebody's bag and shoes were on the floor beside his bed, and Nanci recognized them immediately.

Lola never used the tapestry bags with a fringe that Nanci and all her friends carried. She had a big leather one and she always wore Jesus sandals with the big loop for the toe.

On the bed there was a big blanket that she and Jimmy used when they went to the beach, and it was rumpled, as were the bedclothes.

Nanci could feel the adrenaline pumping but she forced herself to remain calm. She had no idea what she was going to do, but almost as if the sound were coming from another place, she heard herself say, very slowly and deliberately, "She has to leave. I'm going upstairs and when I come back down, she has to be gone."

She couldn't even see Lola. She must be hiding in the bathroom.

Jimmy said, "What am I supposed to do?"

"Jimmy, I don't care what you do"—Nanci could feel herself beginning to lose it—"but she's not staying the night with you."

When she came back down, the shoes and the bag were gone.

Nanci didn't yell at Jimmy. She was surprised at how calm and icy she was, and she could see this shocked Jimmy as much as it had shocked her to find him with another woman. He expected her to yell at him, to shout "You bastard! I'm breaking up with you." But she didn't say a word. She just pulled the sheets off the bed, threw them in the garbage, and remade the bed.

She and Jimmy spent the night in silence.

The next morning Jimmy drove her back to her cottage. He tried to talk to her but she wouldn't answer him. He dropped her off and she went for a long walk along Promised Land to think things over. Weirdly, she felt more betrayed by Lola than by Jimmy. She had trusted this older woman who smoked French cigarettes and had lived all over the place. She had admired her sophistication and wanted to be like her. The only thing she had not admired was the way Lola and her friends slept with each other's partners. She had thought that she and Lola were friends, but in Nanci's mind, friends didn't do that sort of thing to each other. Nanci hadn't seen it coming. Walking along the water's edge, she realized other people must have but had probably not known how to warn her.

On her way back to the cottage she met Mickey, the man who had told her she was beautiful.

Mickey's attracted to you. She remembered Lola's words.

She had discovered he was Jimmy's boss as he had said he might be. Jimmy really liked and admired him.

Nanci smiled at Mickey.

He took her to Merrill's and bought her several drinks. She was unsteady on her feet when they left, and he had to help her along the sandy trail that led to her house—and his.

He was a far more experienced lover than Jimmy, and a part of her could appreciate this. He played her like she was a musical instrument, tuning her body until she was rising and falling in rhythm to his every touch.

It was just one night. Mickey had a girlfriend. And a wife. Nanci knew she would never understand those marriages.

His seduction of her was that of an expert. But who needed an expert? When she woke up beside Mickey, she yearned for the familiar warmth of Jimmy's early morning embrace.

What a way to end her Summer of Love.

FIVE

❧

It was a shock being back in Brooklyn, living at home with their parents after their summer of independence. It had been something of a watershed summer, Nanci reflected. In a way, it marked the turning point in their relationship. To begin with, they were awkward around each other. They had been unfaithful to each other and they both knew it. On the drive back into the city, Nanci had told Jimmy what she had done with Mickey.

For a while, she began to wonder if they would make it back to Brooklyn. Jimmy didn't say a word, just put his foot down on the accelerator and began to drive like a maniac. She knew this was his way of expressing his anger, his hurt, and she also knew that if she tried to remonstrate with him, it would only make it worse. So they rode back in complete silence.

As she got out of the car in front of her parents' house, he realized she was not going to say anything and he leaned over and looked up at her through the car window.

"Okay, I'm angry. You were angry too, about what I did. But we can't let this be the end of us, Nanci. Please."

Nanci nodded. She had guessed that Jimmy would not let her walk away without saying anything. He always wanted to do the right thing. He never liked confrontation.

"Okay. We'll talk. Let's meet up tomorrow."

Yet for a few days they were walking on eggshells, tentative around each other, knowing they had a lot of work to do to get their relationship back to what it had been.

Yet despite what had happened, somehow Nanci was more certain than ever of their love for each other. Out of a potentially disastrous situation came a new closeness. Instead of breaking up, they understood that their experiences with the hippies had taught them something. They learned what it was like to be with other people. If they had never had these two encounters, Nanci realized, they would never have experienced another sexual partner. In the aftermath, when they had talked everything through, Jimmy had told her that until Lola, Nanci was the only girl he had ever slept with. If they had gone on as they were, they might always have wondered . . . and maybe been tempted later on in a more dangerous situation. Lola had been right, in her way, Nanci conceded. It was good to try out different brands before deciding which one suited you best.

But their summer on Long Island also taught them that their life in Brooklyn could not go on as before. They'd been independent all summer, but were still treated as children at home in Brooklyn. The previous night had proved it; they still had someone to answer to.

Nanci had walked into the kitchen with Jimmy just behind her, when her father confronted her in a rage.

"I've been waiting for you to come home! I found these in your bag!" Her father held up her cigarettes. "How many times have I told you you are not allowed to smoke. *How many times?"*

He was shouting in her face. Nanci yelled back, "You're a hypocrite! You smoke twenty a day but I'm not allowed to smoke one. Why don't you practice what you preach?" and then made a run for her room.

This was the problem. They were now nineteen years old but they were still living at home with their parents. They had their dreams but didn't really have a solid plan for the future. Jimmy had started at aeronautical college—a natural progression for a boy who was good at math and who had been to Brooklyn Tech. He should have been studying to be a vet, Nanci thought, but a transit cop with six kids to feed couldn't afford that kind of college tuition.

And what was she going to do? Nanci wondered. Her good Catholic education had programmed her to be a nun, a teacher, a nurse, or a secretary, but she wasn't really interested in any of those things. However, she liked the idea of caring for people in some way, and for this reason she had applied to nursing school and been accepted. Yet it wasn't what she really wanted to do, and when Jimmy's mother, who was a nurse, got her work as a candy striper at Coney Island Hospital, the stark reality of what a nurse actually had to do made

Nanci decide once and for all that nursing wasn't for her. If she was going to care for people, she wanted it to be in a more psychological way than physical.

When she abandoned the idea of going to nursing school, it was a big deal with her parents.

"So what's she going to do?" said Mike De-Serio to Shirley, even though Nanci was sitting right beside him and he could have asked her. "Why did she change her mind?"

"What I really want to be is a writer," Nanci said.

Mike and Shirley looked at her in amazement. Girls did not go off to be writers in Old Mill Basin.

"That's no way to make a living," Mike said.

"Well, at least let me go to community college and study liberal arts," Nanci begged, thinking that they would soon come around and encourage and support her in her determination to be a writer, tell her she was bright and intelligent and that she should take advantage of the fact that English had been her best subject in high school.

But she waited in vain. Mike was too detached and Shirley was much too traditional to imagine that her eldest daughter might want to do something completely different.

Jimmy loved her but he was too busy trying to figure out his own life. Evenings were taken up delivering Chinese food for the Wei-Wei Kitchen. Those were their dates: driving around Brooklyn in his mom's station wagon with a pile of Chinese food in the back. The fun came at the end of the evening when they would return to play ping-pong with the Wei Wei brothers. And find somewhere to make love.

It was hard. The safest place was Jimmy's basement bedroom. His parents worked nights, and she and Jimmy could usually be sure of a couple of hours' privacy, providing they could persuade his little brothers to stay upstairs. Their real problem was Jimmy's grandmother.

She was a Hungarian gypsy and very superstitious. And she liked her bingo. If they could get her to go out to bingo for the evening, they were fine. They would drive her there and pick her up and in between they could be together. But if she decided to stay in, she was at the top of the stairs every five minutes.

"What's going on down there?"

"Nothing, Grandma, just studying."

And the brothers caught on. When they wanted to be really provocative, they waited until Grandma was just about to leave the house for her bingo, then they would shout out, "Good luck, Grandma!"

And she would turn right around and sit down again. If you wished someone good luck, it always brought them bad luck. It was a great way for Jimmy's brothers to tease and torture them.

But even on the nights she was able to lie in Jimmy's arms down in the basement, Nanci knew they were playing with fire.

It was the 1970s and women were coming into their own. Across the Brooklyn Bridge, the New York skyline beckoned with all the excitement that Manhattan had to offer. But Nanci had never had any desire to go to the city. She wanted to get out of Brooklyn, sure, but her dream was to go to the mountains of Vermont or back to the Long Island beaches, not to New York. She didn't want high heels and power suits, she wanted to grow her own vegetables and have a horse and a cow and six kids.

She associated the city with secrets. If you

wanted to hide something from prying eyes in Brooklyn, you went across the bridge to the city.

Like having an abortion.

Nanci had been back in Brooklyn for about a month when she found out her friend Lisa might be pregnant.

"My mom's taking me to this clinic in the city to have a pregnancy test," Lisa confided to Nanci. "Please come with us. I need you with me. You could get your problem checked out at the same time."

Nanci's "problem" was severe menstrual cramps. She had had to stay home so often in high school, she had been advised to get an internal examination. But in Shirley DeSerio's Catholic world, you didn't get that kind of examination until you were married. This was a perfect opportunity, Nanci decided. She'd tell Shirley she was going to the city with Lisa and her mother, and while Lisa was having her pregnancy test, she'd have her exam.

They told her she had a tipped uterus and that it was nothing to worry about. She'd have no problem getting pregnant and by the way, what was she doing about birth control? When they heard that she and Jimmy practiced the rhythm method, she was immediately handed a packet of the Pill.

It was a strange afternoon.

She emerged from her exam to find Lisa sobbing in the waiting room.

"What's the matter?" Nanci asked, putting her arms around her friend. "Is a pregnancy test that painful?"

"I had an abortion," Lisa whispered through her tears. "My mother said I had to."

Nanci was shocked. Lisa's mother had planned it all along but never said a word beforehand. If her daughter turned out to be pregnant, then they would get rid of it there and then.

"But what about Freddie?" Nanci asked, thinking of Lisa's boyfriend. "What's he going to say when he finds out what's happened to his baby?" Nanci couldn't imagine doing anything without discussing it with Jimmy first.

"He's away in the navy. He'll get my letter telling him I might be pregnant and he won't even know the baby is already gone. What have I done?"

"You haven't done a thing," Nanci said gently. "Your mother did this."

There was worse to come. More than anything, Nanci was horrified by the way they were marched off to a restaurant for a plate of spaghetti as if nothing had happened. Lisa was still shaking but her mother was hungry, so that's what they had to do. Suddenly Nanci's mother seemed like an angel.

Late that night, Nanci decided to share the experience with her mother. She knew they were very different in their outlook, but she longed to be closer to Shirley and she was always searching for opportunities to bring them together.

"I have something to tell you," she said to her mom, catching her alone in the kitchen. "I went to a clinic in the city this afternoon and had an internal examination. You know I had to get myself checked out because of my periods. They gave me some birth control pills." She felt nervous but she took them out of her pocket and showed them to her mother.

"Well, you won't be needing those." And in one swift movement, Shirley took them from her daughter's hand and put them in the garbage.

In Shirley's mind there was no sex before marriage, even in the 1970s, so she had closed her mind to the notion of Jimmy and Nanci sleeping together.

So much for trying to get closer to Mom, Nanci thought sadly as she went upstairs to bed.

So they continued using the rhythm method. This is what it must be like playing Russian roulette, Nanci thought each time they made love.

Then one night, in December, three months after they had returned from the Summer of Love, she had a dream.

She saw a little boy with straight black hair and black eyes. He was like the little Indian boy in a picture that hung on the wall in Jimmy's house. In her dream, the little boy was her son.

The next day, sitting on Jimmy's lap in his mother's kitchen, she told him about the dream.

"What does it mean?" he asked her.

"I think it means I'm pregnant. In fact I can just *feel* that I am."

Jimmy's eyes were shining. "Are you sure?"

"Well, I don't *know* for sure, I haven't had a pregnancy test. But my period's late and I have this strange feeling that I am."

He kissed her and rubbed her stomach.

"I think this is so great," he said over and over again, "I think this is so great. *Ooh boy!* We have to tell my mom."

What a different reaction to mine, Nanci thought. *I dread telling my mother but I'll have no problem telling Jimmy's. In fact I want to tell her. She'll know what to do.*

She let Jimmy break the news first and then she joined in the conversation. But mostly she listened quietly as Jimmy's mother offered advice. She had always liked Barbara Jean. She was a warm, capable woman who had always made Nanci feel so welcome in her house.

"You're scared and excited at the same time. Don't worry. We'll arrange for you to have a pregnancy test. Who knows? Maybe you'll get your period tomorrow." She smiled reassuringly. "But if it's confirmed, then you're going to have to tell your mother."

On a freezing January morning, Nanci went back to the same clinic where Lisa had had the abortion. This time, as her eyes scanned the rows of anxious looking women in the waiting room, each one clutching someone's hand for support, Nanci had no doubt what they were there for.

They confirmed her pregnancy. *Do you want an abortion? No, I'm just here for the test.* And she got out of there as fast as she could.

Now there was no getting away from it. She had to tell Shirley

She waited for the right time. It was a weekday, her sisters were in school, her father was at work. Jimmy waited outside as she went in to talk to her mother, who was alone in the kitchen.

"We need to talk about something," Nanci began.

Shirley looked up, her eyes wide in terror. Over the years, Nanci had come to believe that her mother was very intuitive despite her capacity for denial. She seemed to know exactly what she was about to hear.

"Mom, I'm going to have a baby."

Shirley burst into tears. If Nanci had thought for just a second, she could have anticipated this. *Now I've broken her heart*, she thought. This was awful. She wished her mother would yell at her instead.

Eventually she dried her eyes and looked at Nanci, who waited for the kind words of support she had had from Jimmy's mother. *Don't worry. We're going to work this out together.* But all she heard was:

"What are we going to tell your father?"

"We'll tell him I'm pregnant," Nanci said.

"No," Shirley said slowly. She seemed to be working through it in her mind. "You won't tell him. You won't say a word. You will leave here and go to Jimmy's. You will stay there until I call you to come back. You will eat dinner there. Even if you have to spend the night, you will not move until you hear from me. I will speak to your father. If he hears it from you, I don't know what he will do."

Nanci recalled the time her father had exploded in anger when he had discovered her cigarettes. What would he do when he found out she was pregnant?

"Okay, Mom. You're right." Nanci kissed her mother quickly and went outside to where Jimmy was waiting for her.

"I told her," Nanci said.

"Did she freak out?"

"Not really. She cried. She's scared for me, and for herself, I know. All she said was 'What are we going to tell your father?' It was weird."

"How *do* you feel?" Jimmy asked as they

walked around the corner hand in hand to his parents' house.

"I'm not sure," Nanci said. "I've been thinking. I want this baby but I don't want to force you into anything you don't want to do. We have our whole lives ahead of us. We can have a baby later on. We don't have to do anything now."

Jimmy stopped short and turned her around to face him.

"If you're saying what I think you're saying, forget it. I want this baby. I don't want you to have an abortion. Nanci, if you have an abortion, I'll never speak to you again. Never!"

Nanci just stared at him. She watched his eyes. She trusted him. She had been so nervous, but just looking at his sweet face reassured her.

"I told my brother Harold what's happened," he went on. "You know what he said to me? He said, 'If she has an abortion, then you will never marry her.' He said the experience would be so hard on you, it might pull us apart. And you know what? I think he's right." He paused, seemed to take a deep breath, then took both her hands in his. "I want this baby,

CAROLINE UPCHER

Nanci. I want to marry you. We're going to start a family. It's a wonderful thing."

He was proposing to her, Nanci realized. Of all the ways she had imagined he would ask her to marry him, she had never thought it would be like this.

You don't have to do this, she thought. *It's going to change our lives forever.* But what else could they do? They loved each other. They would get married anyway eventually. Jimmy wanted the baby. As he said, it was a wonderful thing.

The atmosphere at his house when they arrived for dinner was so different from hers. All the brothers were gathered at the dinner table and there was a buzz of excitement. They all knew Nanci was going to have a baby. There were no secrets in that house.

Billy and Glenn, the younger boys, didn't say very much. They looked from Jimmy to Nanci and back again, taking it all in—and eating quite a lot of the food, Nanci noticed.

Harry, Tommy, and Bobby were much more verbal. After all, Nanci realized, it could have happened to any one of them. They all had steady girlfriends.

But it hadn't happened to them. It had happened to their younger brother, Jimmy.

"Hey, Jim. How are you going to go from playing hockey on the street to being a dad?" Tommy asked.

"Yeah, and what about finishing college?" Harry added.

"Look"—Jimmy stopped eating and faced them—"I love Nanci. And besides. Can't I play hockey *and* be a father? And there's always night school."

"So what do you think, Nanci?" Bobby asked her.

"Well, what I think is that we *can* do it and our baby will have five terrific uncles, two loving aunts, and you can all babysit for us."

Everyone laughed and suddenly Nanci understood how much Jimmy's brothers cared about him and his future and what it could have been.

Jimmy might be number four in the lineup, but he was still the bravest and most loving man that Nanci knew.

Then Jimmy's father said to Jimmy's mother, "So, they'll move in here with us?" and Jimmy's mother said, nodding, "Yes!"

Nanci was amazed. She knew that history had repeated itself. The same thing had happened with Jimmy's parents—they had had to get married after the conception of his eldest brother—but even so she was surprised that his father was already assuming she would marry Jimmy and move into the LaGarenne household.

He saw her looking at him with his deep blue eyes that were an older and wiser version of Jimmy's. "Listen, Nanci, it's not what I would wish for the two of you, but it's happened, so you'll move in with us. But, Jimmy, you know it's going to be hard. How are you going to support a family?"

He was worried, Nanci saw. He wasn't asking in anger. This was a kind man. He must have had so many dreams for his son's success, and surely none of them had included starting a family at nineteen.

Her eye was on the clock on the wall. Six o'clock passed, then seven and eight. Her father had to be home by now. Had her mother waited until after dinner to tell him? What had happened?

Finally, at eight-thirty, the phone rang. Jimmy answered and handed her the phone.

Her mother's voice sounded desperate. "Nanci, stay where you are," she said.

"Did you tell him? What did he say? How did he take it? Does he want to talk to me?"

"Stay where you are," her mother repeated. "Stay indoors and don't even go to the window. I told your father the minute he came home, and he went beserk. I've never ever seen him in such a rage."

"Mom, are you all right? Should Jimmy and I come over and be with you?"

"*No!*" The urgency in her mother's voice was sending shivers down Nanci's spine. Her eyes met Jimmy's in fear as she heard her mother's voice plead, "Nanci, you have to listen to me. The one person he should not see is Jimmy. I'm frightened of what he might do."

SIX

❧

The next morning, Nanci walked home feeling scared and shaky. What would she do if her father was still home, waiting for her? Jimmy had wanted to come with her, but she had made him stay away.

"It's all right," Shirley said when Nanci slipped in through the kitchen door. "He came home around two in the morning and went straight to sleep. He must have been exhausted. He told me this morning he just walked all over the neighborhood. It was the best thing he could have done. It wore him out."

Nanci felt a wave of relief wash over her. "Is

he still angry? What did he say when you told him?"

But Shirley was evasive. What happened between her and her husband was not Nanci's business. This was the house where nothing was discussed. But Nanci persisted. What had her father said? What was he going to do about the situation?

"He said I had to find out if you were absolutely sure you were pregnant."

"Mom, I told you. I had a pregnancy test."

"Well, you're having another one," Shirley said. "I've made an appointment with my gynecologist, the one who delivered you. He's looked after me, your aunts, and all your female cousins. His is the only word your father will accept. We'll go see him tomorrow."

Nanci hated him on sight.

When she went into his office, the first thing she was aware of was that he smoked. The smell of cigarettes was everywhere.

"So you think you're pregnant?" he challenged her while her mother waited outside.

He had a totally bald head and horrible big hands. He was so rough when he did the examination, Nanci nearly screamed.

Afterwards he went to get her mother.

"She's pregnant," he said to Shirley instead of Nanci.

"She is? Oh my God. So what can we do about this?" Shirley clasped the doctor's arm in her anxiety. Nanci had never seen her look so tense. "We need to take care of it."

Nanci was appalled. Here was her good Catholic mother all of a sudden talking about abortion. "I'm not doing that!" Nanci shouted at her mother.

"Shh, Nanci, be quiet," Shirley said.

"I deliver babies, I don't 'take care' of them," the doctor told Shirley coldly. Now she had made him angry.

"I am not going to have an abortion." Nanci felt herself becoming hysterical. Why couldn't Jimmy be here? She needed him to tell them that was what they wanted. "What are you talking about?" she screamed at her mother. "I thought you were a Catholic. You're only Catholic when it suits you and now it doesn't suit you, well, too bad. How can you suggest such a thing? I am having this baby and we're getting married and *that* is what's happening."

And then Nanci witnessed another first. Shirley lost her cool.

"Will you be quiet, Nanci, just for one minute? You can't get married in a church. What will the neighbors say?"

Nanci opened her mouth to protest, and then shut it again. What was the point? Suddenly she felt exhausted. Here she was with two people who just did not seem to understand what she wanted, who weren't considering her feelings at all.

That was the difference between her mother and Jimmy's. Jimmy's mother was already offering her a home, help with the baby. She didn't care what the neighbors thought.

Nanci went straight there as soon as they left the doctor's office. Barbara Jean had very sweetly stayed home from work to be there for her.

"You know what we have to do, Nanci. We have to sit down with your parents and decide what you're going to do. We'll support you and Jimmy, we'll be there for you, but we all have to face your parents. We have to reach a decision together. This is their grandchild as well as ours."

Nanci knew she was right.

"Please come with me tonight," she asked. "I

don't want to have to face my father without you and Jimmy beside me."

Jimmy came over to her house that night with his parents, and from the minute they walked through the door, the atmosphere was agonizingly tense. Jimmy's mother knew Shirley slightly, but the fathers didn't know each other at all.

Mike DeSerio set out to control the situation right from the start. Jimmy and Nanci sat at one end of the couch by the fireplace, and his parents at the other. On another couch, opposite them, Shirley sat quietly by herself. Neither she nor Jimmy said a word—Shirley, because she never spoke up when Mike was angry, and Jimmy kept quiet because he was scared of instigating any kind of confrontation with Nanci's father.

Nanci's father wouldn't sit down. He was pacing up and down near his wife, jangling the change in his pocket, something he always did when he was nervous.

"This should never have happened, never have happened," he began, facing the La-Garennes.

Nobody said a word.

"Shirley, how come you weren't watching her?" Mike turned on his wife. "You know, it's your fault this has happened. I mean, how in the hell are they going to find the money to support a kid?"

It was exactly what Jimmy's father had asked, but somehow when Mike asked the question, it seemed like he was accusing someone instead of looking for a suggestion.

Again nobody said a word. Nanci felt sorry for her mother. Why did it always have to be her mother's fault? Every time Nanci fell over as a kid, every time she spilled a glass of milk, he turned on Shirley: *Why weren't you watching her?*

Shirley began to cry.

Jimmy's mother sat up. "Look," she said, "it's not the worst thing in the world, it's not something we would have liked to happen, but it has and the good thing is that they love each other."

This enraged Mike even more. "Love, schmove, they don't have a pot to piss in. They don't know what the heck they're doing, they can't blow their own nose. What the hell are they going to do with a kid? She's going to have to take care of it."

Take care of it. Those words again. So that was what he wanted too. It was probably why her mother had behaved the way she had at the gynecologist's. Her husband had decreed that Nanci should get an abortion.

"I will not have an abortion!" Nanci yelled. She was shaking with anger.

"Tell her she has to take care of it," Mike said to Shirley.

Take care of it. Take care of it. Why can't anybody say the word "abortion"? Nanci wanted to scream. It was the same old story. She and Jimmy didn't have names. It was what is *she* going to do about it, what are *they* thinking about? It was as if they were not even in the room.

Nanci could see Jimmy's parents were shocked. Her father was this raving lunatic and her mother was just sitting there crying. Clearly, this wasn't what they had expected at all.

"I won't get rid of my baby!" Nanci was on her feet.

"*Quiet!*" her father yelled back. "This is what she's going to do. She'll take care of it and then we'll have the big wedding."

This was insane. Her father was insisting

that even if she had an abortion, Nanci would have to get married because now they knew she'd had sex.

"No, we won't." Nanci said. "We'll have the baby, that's what we want to do. *And* we'll get married. We love each other, that's what's happening."

"Is she out of her mind? Where are they going to live?" Mike said.

"They can live with us," Jimmy's father replied.

"Like you don't have enough people in your house already?"

Nanci was mortified. It was so tactless, the way her father was implying they'd had too many kids to begin with. How could he talk this way to these people who had been so kind to her?

"Don't talk to them like that! What do you know about what goes on in their house anyway? And since when have you been so interested in my life? All you care about is what the neighbors are going to say. Who cares about me and my baby?"

"*Will you be quiet!*" For the first time he spoke directly to her.

It took three hours before they finally arrived at a decision. Mike DeSerio thought he was controlling everything. He had the stronger personality, but Nanci knew Jimmy's parents had been through this experience with their own first child. They knew what they were talking about and they were firm and persuasive. Nanci was relieved to see that in the end the quiet voice of reason won out. She admired Jimmy's parents so much, the way they supported the argument that Nanci should have the baby, that she and Jimmy should get married, that they should then live with them.

They would get married. In church. But, Mike and Shirley insisted, they had to come up with a story to tell the family. Grandma and the uncles and all the cousins would be told that Nanci and Jimmy had been married two months ago by a justice of the peace, and now it was time for the church wedding. That way they would think Nanci and Jimmy had been married nine months by the time the baby came.

Right, thought Nanci, mentally rolling her eyes.

As expected, when Nanci went to see her, she could tell that her grandmother wasn't fooled for a minute. Nanci sat beneath the picture of the Pope on her grandmother's pantry door, nibbling the homemade cookies her grandmother always baked, and she nearly choked when Grandma said, "Nanci, you have to go somewhere and take care of it."

Nanci couldn't believe her ears. Forget about her mom and dad, now her eighty-year-old Catholic grandmother was advocating abortion. Would the hypocrisy never end?

On the other hand, she had to admire her grandmother. Nunziata DeSerio was the only person who had the upper hand over Mike De-Serio, the only person who challenged him except, Nanci realized, herself. For the first time she felt something in common with the woman for whom she had been named. Deep down Nanci knew she had inherited the old woman's fiery, independent spirit and that it was something she would probably thank her for as time went by.

You're a tough old woman, Grandma, she thought, *but now I'm even tougher, and I'm going to have this baby no matter what.*

$\mathcal{N}$ow that it was decided they were going to be married, the wedding would take place as soon as possible.

There wasn't time to do much, but she had to at least find a dress.

Nanci hadn't been shopping with her mother since she was a little girl. It was a time when she used to feel like a grown-up, riding on the city bus to A&S in downtown Brooklyn to have her day with her mom. They always had a chicken salad sandwich in the little restaurant, and then they'd wander through the store. It was a treat she had always looked forward to.

This shopping trip would not be so carefree, of course. There was no point getting a traditional wedding dress for what was going to be a very quick wedding. There would be no invitations, no flowers in the church, only bouquets for herself and her maid of honor. Nanci didn't even have an engagement ring, not that she minded. She didn't care much about material things, really. Nature, the outdoor world, was much more important to her. She had always assumed she would get married on the beach.

But she had to have a dress, so off she went with Shirley. This time they went to Macy's in Brooklyn. It was somehow fitting that they didn't even try to re-create those special days of childhood by heading to A&S.

Nanci had her heart set on something antique, so she chose a cream-colored dress instead of white, which, under the circumstances,
was probably just as well. It was the middle of
winter, so it had to be warm. And it had to fit
Nanci's two-months-pregnant figure. They
found a long dress with a ruffle around the bottom. It had a high neck and long sleeves and an
embroidered area in the bodice that was see-
through. It was very pretty in an almost vin-
tage, Victorian way, very demure. And it cost
under fifty dollars.

Jimmy didn't own a suit. For the senior
prom he had worn a rented tuxedo. His friends
had teased him and called it the tuxedo that
matched the rug. It was not quite brocade and
not quite tapestry but something in between,
and quite by chance it had matched the rug at
the Terrace on the Park in Queens, where the
prom was held. The senior prom seemed a long
time ago as Jimmy went off on his own shopping spree to Max's Men's Store and bought
himself a brand-new brown suit.

And then everything began to happen very
fast. A couple of weeks later—although it

seemed to Nanci as if it were only a couple of days—they had their wedding.

Nanci went to the church in her uncle's old red Buick. Jimmy was waiting for her at the top of the aisle. She thought he looked very handsome in his new suit. She had parted her hair in the middle and taken two tiny strands from the front and braided them. They were tied in a white ribbon at the back of her head, and her long dark hair fell down her back to her waist.

Her mother looked immaculate as always. For the service, she wore a black suit with a plunging neckline, and for the dinner afterwards, she changed into a sparkling silver jersey knit top. Nanci thought her father looked like something out of a Mafia movie. He had mournful saturnine good looks and his black hair was slicked back off his face. But it was the bright red shirt and white tie that he wore under his dark suit that made him look like a member of the mob. Her sister Linda was her maid of honor in a long red dress, and Jimmy's brother Billy was his best man in a plaid jacket. There were no flowers, no boutonnieres, no music, no ribbons on the pews, and the church was almost empty. It was a bitterly cold day in

February, there was snow on the ground, and if anyone other than the wedding party dressed up for the ceremony, it was only to bundle up against the cold in a sheepskin jacket.

It was nothing like the wedding they had dreamed of. Afterwards, there was a dinner in a restaurant, but no merriment and dancing.

Yet Nanci didn't really notice. She could tell Jimmy felt the same. They were in a separate place, seeing only each other. They were just so happy to be getting married.

And of course there was no honeymoon. Just a couple of nights in a borrowed apartment. The big excitement was a TV on a trolley they could wheel from room to room. Mostly, it stayed with them in the bedroom.

In spite of everything, Nanci thought it was romantic because Jimmy was so sweet.

They lay in bed and held each other and talked about how everything had changed from what they had envisioned.

"It wasn't what we planned but at least we had a wedding." Nanci rubbed her belly. "I can't wait to feel him kick."

"How do you know it's a he?"

"I just do."

"You know something, Nanci? Someday we

will get married on the beach. And I will always take care of you. You know that, don't you?"

She nodded. She knew that whatever happened, he would always be there.

He began by taking care of the grocery shopping. The most outstanding memory Nanci would retain of her first days of married life was the sight of her new husband coming through the door, staggering under the weight of the groceries. There were just the two of them, and they would only be there for two days, but Jimmy came back from the store with the largest containers he could find of mayo, mustard, juice, as well as a giant chicken and several gallons of milk. Bulk-buying for a family of six boys was the only way he knew how to shop. *Things are going to have to change,* Nanci thought. *From now on there's just me and him.*

And the baby.

SEVEN

"*Drive!*" Nanci screamed. She was lying in agony on the back seat of the car. Her contractions were coming every two minutes.

"Okay, honey, take it easy. We'll get you there. Don't worry." Her father reached over from the passenger seat and patted her head.

Her father!

Who would ever have thought that her father would be sitting there beside Jimmy as they drove her to the hospital? Nanci could not get over the change in him since the wedding. It was as if now he had nothing left to fight with her about, he had given up and decided to be nice. It proved Nanci's belief that everyone had a good side buried inside them. It only

CAROLINE UPCHER

needed a certain situation to bring it to the surface. The imminent arrival of his first grandchild seemed to have done the trick for Mike
DeSerio. As it turned out, they didn't move in
with Jimmy's parents. They found a little
apartment they could just barely afford, and
from the minute they moved in, Nanci's father
had been there to help. *Do you need a hand with
the painting? Here's money for the crib. Here's
money for the pram.*

Jimmy couldn't believe it. "I don't need
that," he'd said one day late in the pregnancy,
when Nanci's father handed him five hundred
dollars.

Mike waved it in his face. "Take it. I
wouldn't give it to you if I didn't want you to
have it."

"Thank you," Jimmy said meekly while
Nanci looked on, happy to see a relationship at
last beginning to flourish between her husband
and her father.

"He means well," Jimmy said to her that
night. "He's not in touch with his emotions but
he's the kind of guy who's always going to be
there to take care of his family in a manly way,
like with money. It's the only way he knows
how."

It was hot as hell. Nanci had walked around Brooklyn with a loose shirt covering her huge belly. She was happy they had found a new apartment close to her mother. She didn't agree with her mom's choices, but regardless, it was good to have family close by. They had started out married life in an apartment house that faced an empty lot, and at night Nanci looked out of the window to an expanse of darkness that was spooky. Jimmy was out at night school and she was alone with her unborn baby. Son of Sam had terrorized the area, killing women with long dark hair. Back then she had never left the house without a hood over her head.

They had no air conditioning, just a fan. Some days she'd get so hot, she'd have to go to her mother's and flop like a whale in the little plastic pool that stood above ground in her mother's eight-by-ten backyard, the one she had played in all her life.

Visiting a house full of women when she was pregnant felt like the right thing to do. Besides, she felt guilty about the way things had turned out. She wanted to reach out to her mother in some way and establish a new relationship with her. There was a surprise shower, gifts of used baby clothes with everyone on the block contributing. And her mother became so much closer, sitting quietly sewing a quilt for the baby, with the name Nanci had chosen stitched in the corner: Jason.

"It's not an Italian name," Grandma DeSerio complained. She couldn't even pronounce it. "How you call him? Jaso?"

*W*hen they finally reached the hospital, Nanci felt she was being punished for all her sins in one long session. The baby was to be delivered by the bald-headed ob-gyn who had confirmed her pregnancy, the one who smoked. She had asked him about the Lamaze method, but he had told her, "Honey, you don't want to be a martyr, we'll give you pills. You'll be knocked out."

But where were the pills? Nobody gave her anything for what seemed like forever. A little while later, she woke up in the middle of an intense contraction, hooked up to a monitor and all alone.

"*Jimmy!*" she screamed. "*Where are you? I need you!*"

This was not at all what she had planned. She had always dreamed that the birth of her first child would be a very natural thing, with Jimmy by her side holding her hand. But just as her dream wedding had never happened, so her first birth experience turned into a nightmare.

"He has to wait outside." A nurse who looked like a prison warden came into the room. "Doctor won't let him in the room." The nurse was shaving her roughly. "You have a beauty mark right below your pubic hair. How come you never told me? I could have shaved it off."

How did I know to tell her? Nanci wondered.

Jimmy wasn't allowed near her no matter how much she cried for him. The doctor brought a team of students in to take a look at her. How come they were allowed in and Jimmy had to wait outside? Nanci felt horrible and degraded. She was in labor for fourteen hours. There was endless talk of a cesarean but the bald-headed doctor waited and waited until the situation grew truly dangerous. Then he went in with forceps. Jason was born with a lump on his head as a result.

But he was worth every minute of the agony. Nanci held him in her arms and thought he was beautiful. He had a mass of jet black hair, big black eyes in a little round face. He was exactly like the child in her dream.

If she had been punished before, now she was being rewarded. Not only was Jason the perfect baby who liked to sleep all the time—and always right through the night—but Jimmy turned out to be the perfect father.

She was breast-feeding but her sweet baby Jason was having trouble sucking, and her breasts were engorged. The milk wasn't coming through, and in her struggles, her stitches broke. The La Leche League turned up to lecture her on how she must keep breast-feeding even though she was in intense pain. But they hadn't anticipated running into a father like Jimmy.

"You're going to have to leave," he told them. "Can't you see my wife is having problems? It's hurting her. I'm going to take care of the feeding from now on."

He worked all day. In the evening he went to school. Yet he always found time to help, to run errands.

"I'm going out to the store. We need formula," he'd say.

In the middle of the night he got up and fed

the baby. It was as if he never slept; his ear was constantly attuned to the sound of Jason waking up.

Those first few months, Nanci longed for privacy. Since she had had the baby, she and Jimmy didn't seem to have any time to themselves. It wasn't Jason who intruded. He slept all the time. Her sister came around with her camera, and Jimmy's brothers dropped by unannounced whenever they felt like it.

Jimmy finally threw them out, just as he had the La Leche League.

"But we're family," they protested. "We want to see the baby."

"Yeah," Jimmy said, "and you think you can just drop by because now I have a place of my own and you want to hang out in it. Listen, I'm married now and you have to respect that. You want to come by, call first."

"Thank you for that," Nanci said, drawing him to her in bed that night. "I love how you're so proud to be married, so proud to be a father."

"I told you I'd take care of you," Jimmy whispered. "Now I'd better get some sleep before Jason wakes up and wants his bottle."

Nanci lay awake, smiling in the darkness.

She remembered her determination to have a relationship different than her father's and mother's. She had found one, she had her little family all to herself. As soon as she recovered from the trauma of Jason's birth, she would be as happy as a person could expect to be.

For the first three years of their marriage, while Jason was still very young, Nanci worked hard to keep everything as romantic as possible. They would have candlelit dinners at home while Jason slept beside them.

Her days were as idyllic as they could be without Jimmy by her side. She would take Jason out for long walks in his carriage with the other mothers in the neighborhood, and later on she put him in a bike seat and rode with him to Marine Park.

On the weekends, their friends Joe, Gail, and Julie often came over for jam sessions, singing while Jimmy played guitar.

But her favorite time of the year was the summertime, when she went out to stay at Jimmy's grandparents' house on Long Island. Jimmy joined them on weekends, and Jason took his first steps into the clear blue water of the bay. He was the perfect child. As a baby he had slept so much, sometimes she stood over him to make sure he was still breathing. Then he walked and talked early, when he was little more than a year.

Nanci often wondered if these years of blissful young married fun would have continued if, in 1980, their building had not been sold.

For eighty thousand dollars they could have bought the whole house and rented out their apartment. But they didn't have that kind of cash, nor did their parents.

They searched and searched but they could not find a place to rent on Jimmy's salary, so there was nothing else to do but move in with Jimmy's parents, all three of them sleeping in the same room.

This time there was nothing Jimmy could do to secure them any privacy except put up a curtain between their bed and Jason's. How could you have any privacy with a three-year-old sleeping in the same room?

They ate dinner with the family every night. Their business was everybody's business.

It was only a matter of time before they had their first big argument and everybody knew about it.

They had been living with his parents for a

year. She had gone Christmas shopping and found a book called *One Child by Choice*.

"Why are you reading that?" Jimmy asked when he saw it.

"It's brilliantly written and I can relate to this woman's story. It's exactly how I feel. You can have a great marriage with just one child and—"

"Are you serious? You can't possibly believe that. My mother had six kids."

"I know, Jimmy, but I'm not ready to have another child yet."

"So you're not saying you don't want any more children?"

"I don't know. I'm not sure," she said. She was torn. They could barely afford one child as it was, and there was never any privacy. Why should they have more so soon?

But Jimmy didn't see it in quite such a practical light. They were living in his parents' house, where he felt more at home than she. He didn't mind the circumstances of their lives as much as she did.

"What do you mean, you're not sure?"

"I mean what I say. I'm not ready to think about it. I had a horrific time giving birth to Jason. I'm not sure I want to go through that again. We're fine as we are."

Now Jimmy was getting angry. "Look at that kid across the street, he's an only child and he's so lonely. Jason needs to have brothers and sisters."

"Jimmy, not now, I can't—"

"I grew up with five brothers. You grew up with two sisters. What are you thinking of?" he said, truly mystified.

She was thinking of *them*, of their marriage, couldn't he see that? She was thinking of herself and Jimmy and how they needed to be alone together. The minute he had stepped back into his parents' house, he had reverted to being one of the brothers. She had to make him understand that instead of adding another member to the family, they needed to get away from the crowd.

"Hey, Nanci, he's right," said Billy. "You want more than one child."

"How come you don't want a big family?" said Harry. "What's wrong with all of us?"

"Nanci, what's the matter with you?" piped in Bobby, "Jason needs brothers just like his father did."

This was the reason she had to get away. She wasn't just having an argument with her husband, she was taking on his whole damn family. But she was determined to win. She wasn't Nunziata DeSerio's granddaughter for nothing. She might be a woman contesting six brothers, but if she didn't at least try to make Jimmy understand, what was the point of being married?

"It's not just that I'm scared of giving birth again. I know that was three years ago, and the truth is, it's more than that. We need to move out of here, Jimmy. We need to be a couple again, a tiny unit like we used to be. Just us. And Jason. And then, when we're back where we were, when we're a pair of lovers again instead of two people sharing a room with a child, then we can start thinking about having more kids."

Jimmy's eyes seemed to soften.

She went on, "You are the most important thing in my life. You, my husband, my lover. Diapers, tiny-tot play groups, strollers, all those things will never squeeze you out of my heart. There'll always be room for you there. You know that, don't you? But I don't want to be one of those women who changes from a wife into a mother. I want to be both. We can't lose *us*."

"I'll speak to my mother tomorrow," he told her, and she breathed a sigh of relief. She loved him so much. She knew she hadn't totally convinced him, that he would hate to leave his family. But he would go along with what she said because he loved her. He would show her that even though they disagreed, she was the most important thing in his life too. Just as he had promised on their wedding night, he would always be there to take care of her.

They found an apartment right across the street from where Jason would go to school. It had brown walls and bright orange shag carpet. It was truly hideous but the landlord didn't understand when they ripped it out and stenciled all over the walls. "That's good carpet, what are you doing?" he asked every time he came to their door and took a peek to see what they were doing.

But they had to make the place their own.

The great thing about having their own apartment again was that Nanci got to spend more time with Jason. She felt bad about leaving Barbara Jean's house. In spite of everything, the brothers had been so good to her, they almost felt like the brothers she never had. The house had always been a friendly place, the coffeepot was always on, neighbors were always dropping by. And Jason had had all these people to entertain him. He was the only grandchild and the center of attention.

But now she was on her own with him again. Had she done the right thing? Only time would tell, but at least she was rediscovering her son.

He was so inquisitive and she could see early on that he was highly intelligent. But perhaps the best thing was that he seemed to have inherited her own love of books. She sat with him every day, showing him books, and realized that soon he would be able to read, maybe even as early as four or five.

Now he was going to prekindergarten and Jimmy was going out to play hockey several times a week. Nanci sat home alone on those nights, and even though she tried her best to banish it, the old restlessness started to resurface.

What is the matter with me? she thought. *I have everything I wanted and yet somehow I'm still searching for something more. I just don't feel stretched.*

She was in limbo. She had opted to be a stay-at-home mom, and she didn't have a problem with that. But just because she wanted to devote some time to raising her child didn't mean that was all there was to life. On the other hand, she didn't aspire to being an eighties corporate woman in a power suit.

She knew Jimmy was trying to figure out who he was too. Here he was, married with a family though none of his friends were. But Jimmy didn't spend time brooding about how he was going to find himself. She sometimes wondered if she was doing all his worrying for him.

He worked at a firm of aerospace engineers. He was involved in making fighter planes for the government. How did that happen? Nanci asked herself. That wasn't who Jimmy was, Nanci knew. He shouldn't be working with fighter planes instead of animals just because they needed the money.

She tried to keep her fretting to herself. Jimmy worked so hard and was always so good-natured about it. It didn't seem fair that she should be at home, reaping all the benefits, and still feel restless.

The one thing that always helped her work

her way through these low spots was to sit down and write about it.

One night she wrote a short story about a woman who ran an antique shop, and sent it off to *Redbook*. Even if *Redbook* rejected it, somehow she had found the writing process satisfying, as if some kind of inner demon were being exorcised.

"Why don't you take a course in creative writing at Brooklyn College?" Barbara Jean suggested, trying to cheer her up when *Redbook* sent it back. "They have courses in everything—cabinet refinishing, belly dancing—you can do writing."

Nanci leapt at the idea, but it was a weekend course, which meant she wasn't home on Saturdays.

"How can you not be here on Saturdays?" Jimmy was amazed. He worked all week and then when he was at home on the weekend, she was gone. She came home and found him searching in the refrigerator for something to eat. "I'm happy for you that you're studying creative writing, but does it have to be on a Saturday?"

She felt a little twinge of guilt. She had to admit that she wanted to do some things that were just for her, all the things that having Jason had made her put on hold. Meanwhile, Jimmy was making fighter planes to support them. It was crazy.

At least she was still putting him first where it mattered. When he came home at night and Jason was sleeping, she lit candles, opened a bottle of wine, and put on her Victoria's Secret nightgown. At the center of their marriage, they still had their love. They would muddle through, albeit each with their own frustrations.

*U*ntil the day Jason's kindergarten teacher called and they had their next big argument.

"I need you and your husband to come to a parents' meeting," she said. "We have a problem with Jason."

Jimmy wouldn't go.

"What's the big deal? You go. I'm going out to hockey."

"Jimmy, she asked for both of us. I need you with me."

"Listen, my mom had six kids. She went to all the school meetings; she went to all the Boy Scouts stuff. My dad never went to anything; he worked two jobs, sometimes three. He never had time to go to the school. I don't have time either."

"What does that have to do with anything?" Nanci yelled. "My father didn't come to my school either, but we're not our parents. We're Jason's parents and it's important." She couldn't believe he was right there in front of her in the bedroom, putting on his hockey equipment, lacing up his pads, when they could see the school all lit up for the meeting right across the street.

"Listen," he yelled back, "I need time to play hockey. I need time off from this family thing. None of the guys I work with are married. When they're done with work, they get to go out and have fun and I have to . . ."

He stopped. The rest of the sentence hung unspoken between them. *I have to come home to my wife and kid.* Nor did she say, *You were the one who wanted to get married and have a baby, Jimmy. I suggested an abortion but you wouldn't hear of it.*

She hadn't wanted to have an abortion either, but she hadn't wanted them to be so tied down with a baby. Their dreams of peace and love in the Rocky Mountains were well and truly crushed now. There was no going back.

She stormed out of the house and walked

across the road to the school. As she entered the parents' meeting, she knew it was going to be one of the worst nights of her life. All the other fathers were there.

"Where's your husband?" Jason's teacher asked her in front of everyone.

"He had to go to night school," Nanci lied.

"Well," said the teacher when Nanci went in to meet with her, "your husband really should be here to listen to this. Your son, Jason, you have to do something about him. He doesn't listen in class. He's too outspoken for his own good. He's trouble. If he doesn't start to quiet down, he's going to have some very serious problems. I think you should consider therapy."

Nanci clutched the arms of the chair she was sitting in to stop herself from crying out in shock.

It was true, now he had turned six, Jason was growing into something of a handful. He was so intelligent, with such an inquiring mind, that sometimes it was hard to keep him amused. But weren't teachers supposed to be able to deal with children like this?

Nanci couldn't believe that Jason had to be in class with this seemingly hostile woman every day. What came at Nanci like machine gun fire was: *Doesn't listen . . . too outspoken . . . trouble . . . serious problems . . . consider therapy . . . goodbye.* The woman didn't seem to be at all concerned that she was delivering shocking news to a mother. There was no softening of the blow. At that moment, Nanci hated her for her lack of sensitivity.

And she couldn't discuss it further because there were other parents waiting for their turn in the hallway outside. Couples. Mothers *and fathers.*

Nanci was livid. She went home, tossed a couple of bucks to Jimmy's little brother Glenn, who was babysitting, picked up Jason and left the house. She took a taxi to their old friend Joe Imbriale's house. He was no longer living with his mother, Marie, in the house where Jimmy had first asked her out. Now he was married with a house of his own.

Jimmy called at one o'clock in the morning to see where she was. He'd called her mother, his mother, all their friends. When Joe answered the phone, Nanci could tell he was between a rock and hard place, because if anything he was more Jimmy's friend than hers.

"Calm down," she heard him say. "Don't come over here angry, that's the worst thing you can do. She needs to calm down and so do you. Jason's fine."

To her surprise, Jimmy took the next day off from work. He was waiting for her when she got home.

"We need to talk," he said.

"Damn right," she said, and told him what the teacher had said about Jason.

"We have to do something," he said.

"I'm going to go to the school tomorrow and take him out of that witch's classroom right away. And by the way," she went on, "I am not going to put up with that kind of excuse for not coming with me to the school. You are not your father and I am not your mother. I am not going to have six children like I said I wanted to when we were kids. And you don't work all the time and not have time for Jason."

Jimmy was nodding slowly as she talked, as if he understood everything she was saying. Once or twice he opened his mouth to speak, but she held up her hand.

"Let me finish. You're not like your father. He never had time for you guys. You play with Jason all the time, you're a terrific father, so don't try and pretend you're not. I need you and we don't have the kind of relationship where you go off and play hockey when I need you."

"I'm sorry," Jimmy said, "nothing should stand in the way of my being a good father."

"And a good husband," she added.

"I try to be a good husband."

She looked at him and he looked so sad. He had no animals, just machine parts to look forward to at work. And he loved his father. He might know that he had not been there for him, but it hurt him to acknowledge it.

Suddenly she realized she needed to do something for him.

"You need a break," she said. "Why don't we leave Jason with my mother and go out to your parents' house at the beach for the weekend?"

"But it's October. It'll be cold out there."

"So? We'll keep each other warm."

Barbara Jean hugged her when Nanci asked her if they could use the house.

"Of course you can. It's the best thing you could do. And don't worry about Jason. What you should do is send him to a Montessori school. He's a creative little boy—like his mother. He's precocious and he's intelligent and my guess is he'll always be a handful, but at Montessori he'll have four teachers instead of one and he'll be allowed to speak up and be himself."

And when she heard those words, Nanci began to have a little hope.

It was cold at Jimmy's parents' house on Long Island. For one thing, the house was located in an exposed position, right on the end of a point, with nothing but flat wetlands all around it. For another, there was no heating. His parents used it only as a summer home. One day they would retire out here and until that time they didn't see the point of spending money to install heating.

And, as Nanci and Jimmy learned from the bulletins on the radio, there was a nor'easter on the way. Nanci wondered if they should leave, but Jimmy thought they'd be okay.

"But we have to take it seriously," Jimmy said. "Sometimes a nor'easter can be worse than a hurricane. It's the worst kind of storm. Fill the bathtub with water. I'll fill as many pots and pans as I can find. We're going to need all the water we can get if the power goes out."

"Doesn't it get flooded if there's a lot of rain?" she asked.

"Sure, but that's the fun part. They'll come and rescue us in these great big amphibious cars that literally drive across the water."

When the storm started, Nanci was frightened. The forked lightning seemed to split the dark sky over the water outside, and with the torrential rain that followed came the wind. It howled relentlessly around the little house.

"They say it's going to get up to fifty, sixty miles an hour. There's dogs and cats and wildlife out there," Jimmy said. "You're scared, so think what it must be like for them. I'd like to open the door and invite them all inside where they can be safe."

The power went out around nine o'clock at night. They had already eaten dinner and there was nothing left to do except go to bed with a little kerosene heater burning away beside them. But when they began to make love, the bed frame creaked so loudly, it threatened to drown out the wind outside.

"It's going to collapse any minute unless we take it easy," Nanci giggled.

"Well, I'm not in the mood to take it easy,"

Jimmy whispered, "but I have an idea. Get up and I'll show you."

He dragged the mattress off the bed and into the living room, where he laid it down on the floor in front of the fireplace. Nanci went around the house searching for candles, holding a hurricane lantern high above her head for light. She pushed the candles into bottles and candlesticks and placed them on the floor all around the mattress. Jimmy made a big fire with logs and kindling.

Together, they lit the fire and the candles and stood holding hands and looking into each other's eyes while the firelight bathed their bare skin in a warm glow. Nanci let her fingers begin to wander over Jimmy's body, and when he did the same, his infinitesimal touch aroused her nerve ends to an almost unbearable fever. They climbed under the blankets on the mattress in front of the roaring fire with an urgency that matched the flames behind them.

"Kiss me," Nanci begged, "come inside me . . . now!" She didn't know if it was the wind or her heart that was creating the rushing in her ears. All she knew was that it was exciting, more exciting than she had ever known it to be with Jimmy.

They made love throughout the night, rising only to stoke the fire and put on another log. The candles burned lower and lower and Jimmy rose above her to crane his neck and blow them out one by one. Then they were lying in each other's arms with just the burning embers glowing in the dark behind them.

They were exhausted but they couldn't sleep. The storm was dying down and they snuggled up to each other to watch the dawn come up outside.

"I wish we could always be here. I wish we could live out here," Nanci said.

"It's what I've always wanted, ever since I started coming out here as a kid," Jimmy said. "Who knows, maybe one day we will."

What's to stop us? Nanci wondered. But she knew the answer. Same as always. Money. This was his parents' house. How would they ever afford one of their own in one of the most expensive areas of real estate in the state of New York?

"Do you think we just made a baby?" she asked.

She felt Jimmy shift a little. "I'm not getting

into this," he said. "We've had this argument. You know what I want. I heard what you told me. I want to wait until you're ready. I want to try to understand."

"But Jimmy, I think I am ready," she told him.

He raised himself on his elbows and looked down at her.

"Did I hear you correctly?"

She nodded.

"What's made you change your mind?"

"Because now I feel like I have control over it. I want the experience of planning another baby, choosing to get pregnant because I feel ready."

"You make me so happy." Jimmy kissed her and it was as if the words had relaxed him; he finally fell asleep in her arms.

Nanci wondered if the wind was listening to them down the chimney. Would it answer their prayers of love and bring them another child?

The next morning was drenched in brilliant sunshine. The blue water stretching across the bay was so still after the storm that Nanci hoped desperately that she had conceived. For the peace and calm that lay before her as she looked out from the deck was the perfect moment for her baby to start its unborn life.

EIGHT

❦

*F*or a while Nanci found she could begin to dream again.

Eric, born in July, was an adorable baby. Nanci knew she had done the right thing in suggesting the weekend at the beach. She had worked out that a marriage needed an injection of romance every so often. And now she and Jimmy were more in love than ever. They were twenty-six, still very much the young married couple, but providing she did everything she could to keep their love alive, she knew they could be happy within their little family unit.

Maybe she didn't like the fact that Jimmy was making A10 fighter planes when she knew that what he really wanted to do was take care of animals, but at least now he was working for a company where he was being paid much more money. Maybe they could begin to save for the life they had dreamed about.

Until he got laid off.

Maybe this is a sign, she thought. *Maybe it means we should take off. We're free to go on the road now, like we always wanted to.*

"What about my degree?" Jimmy said. "I've worked hard for that and I want to use it."

He had continued aeronautic school at night and had acquired a degree in airframe engineering, which meant he was qualified to work as a mechanic on commercial airlines.

Except now there were no jobs.

"Everyone says I should take the fireman's test," Jimmy said at supper one night.

"Are you crazy?" Nanci said, "That's a single guy's job. They sleep there, they eat there, they cook there, they work three days in a row before they come home. I'd never see you, Jimmy, and I couldn't bear that."

"I know, I know." He put his arm round her and drew her to him, trying to calm her down. "It might not be so bad. I might work nonstop but then they have four days off."

"Maybe," she said, only slightly mollified.

"But I just don't think it's the best job for a family man."

"Well," Jimmy said, "this family man has to feed a wife and two kids, so I'm going to take the test no matter what you say."

He passed it with flying colors.

"You become a fireman and you and me, we're not happening anymore," Nanci said. "Having a husband who is a fireman is just not conducive to marriage. I said that before you took the test."

Jimmy looked at her.

"You really mean that, don't you?"

"Absolutely." Nanci was firm. She didn't want to be too controlling, she didn't want to lay down the law. She wanted him to understand why she didn't want him to become a fireman and to decide for himself what to do.

"Nanci, you're right. I can see that. I'll try to think of something else. But it's scary, you know? Being unemployed and wanting to take care of you and the boys."

"I know," she said. "I understand. Believe me, I do. But we have to think long term. We'll get through this."

She loved him for listening to her over the fireman issue. But her father didn't get it at all.

"You shouldn't listen to her," Mike DeSerio said, when they went to dinner with her parents. "You want to become a fireman, become a fireman. What does she know about it?"

"We don't have that kind of marriage," Jimmy told him. "I wouldn't do something Nanci didn't want me to do."

Mike DeSerio shook his head in bewilderment. This was not a marriage he understood.

But the other thing everyone said to Jimmy was "Take the police test." And Jimmy had an idea. When he was going to aeronautics school at La Guardia airport, he had met a man who had become one of their closest friends. Nanci remembered the day Jimmy had met him.

"This guy walks into the room and says his name is Charlie Trojan and I thought he had to be joking, like he was named after a brand of condoms? But he came and sat right down next to me. I had never met the guy before and suddenly here he is laughing and joking like we've known each other for years."

And when she met him, Nanci loved him too. He was one of those guys who just laughed when things went wrong. He always looked on the bright side of life. And he was cute looking, Nanci thought, rather like Kevin

Bacon. Women loved him. When they all went to parties together, Charlie was always at the center of a group of women.

"He loves life, that guy," Jimmy said.

"Yes, and we love him," Nanci said.

"So," Jimmy said to Nanci, "here's my idea: Charlie's a cop but he's in this aviation unit. He's a pilot. With my experience and my degree, maybe I can be in that unit."

"No, please don't tell me you are going to be a cop," Nanci pleaded.

"You have to trust me on this, Nanci. I'm going to talk to your father. He's a lieutenant, maybe he can help swing it that I get into that aviation unit."

"Oh, Jimmy, no! Think of our dreams. We always said we didn't want to turn out like our parents. This is our life. Do you really see us as a cop and his wife?"

Nanci knew she was making life difficult for him, and she felt dreadful, but she couldn't help it. It was because she loved him and she wanted the best for him that she had to speak out.

"Listen, Nanci, let me explain." She could see Jimmy was as unhappy as she was. "Number one, yes, it's true, my dad was a cop and I always said I didn't want to be one. But we have to face up to the fact that our lives have just not turned out the way we thought they would. Of course we had our dreams and we always will. But they have to be dreams for the future, because we have these two little boys. Now, I'm mad as hell that I didn't think to try and become a zookeeper when I was nineteen, before you got pregnant. But I didn't and we got married and I have a boy and a newborn baby to take care of. Didn't I always promise you I'd take care of you?"

Nanci nodded. She knew what was coming. Jimmy always had to do the right thing. She loved him because he was decent and honorable, but it looked as if these very qualities were going to crush everything they had dreamed about.

"I want to be a cop because I'm thinking of you, Nanci, I'm thinking of the benefits for my family. I'm thinking of the twenty-year retirement plan. I can be out in twenty years and then we can do what we want."

"Twenty years!" repeated Nanci, almost in tears. "The boys will be grown up by then."

"Understand what I'm saying." Jimmy knelt

beside her, took her hand. "I'm not proposing I become a New York City cop on patrol. That wouldn't be a good choice as a father and husband. That's one of the hardest jobs anybody could ever do. You never know, when you walk into any situation, whether it's two people arguing or a burglary, you could be killed. It's a tough job, it really is." He was speaking in a low voice; he sounded earnest and strong. "But I'm talking about aviation, I'm talking about helping people, doing medevacs, searching for people in the river, lost kids, people who jump off the Brooklyn Bridge, people in accidents, air-sea rescue. I'm not going to be one of the lost souls, those cops walking the beat. Or those cops who show up, get in the car, and answer as few calls as possible because they're so fed up with the job. My work's going to be worth doing because I'll be a pilot."

Nanci fought back the tears. She could see that Jimmy needed this. She wouldn't be able to sway him as she had when he had talked about becoming a fireman. And she saw that she had to support him, to bury her anxiety about the police force and be there for him.

Later he talked to Mike DeSerio, and of

course her father said, "Sure, I'll help you, Jimmy. You went to aeronautical college, you can get in as a helicopter mechanic."

He's going to be a pilot, he's not a cop, he's going to be a pilot and that's okay, Nanci told herself over and over again while Jimmy was in the police academy. As she fed and cared for the newborn Eric, she repeated the mantra over and over.

And she could see he was enjoying himself despite the fact that he wasn't a boot camp kind of a guy. He'd never been in the military, and a sergeant yelling right in his face, telling him what to do, was something he couldn't handle. He'd always had a big mouth and he wasn't afraid to use it, so when he came home at night and told her stories, Nanci just smiled. She could just imagine the scene.

"We had to elect a company sergeant and they asked, 'Who has military experience?' So this guy is picked just because he was in the military. Of course he immediately starts acting like a hard-ass with all these kids who can't run and they can't do the push-ups. I told him, 'Do you realize when you get out of the police academy you're going to be on the street working alongside these very same guys and they're going to remember you yelled at them. What if you get shot and one of them is your partner? Don't you think it would make more sense to encourage them rather than yell in their faces?' "

And there were women at the academy.

"They put me in the ring with a woman," said Jimmy one day. "I'm supposed to box with her and she's like five foot nothing."

Nanci smiled again, remembering how when she had first met Jimmy he was this little shrimp of a guy. "Skinny like a pencil," was the phrase everyone had used to describe him. Now he was a big guy, six foot two.

"So I'm being real gentle with her, I'm saying, 'Here's what you do, I'll teach you how to punch.' So the instructor comes over and he says, 'What are you doing? You have to hit her back real hard.' So I said, 'Are you kidding me?' He says, 'You don't hit her back, I'm going to hit you.' "

Nanci smiled. She could just imagine it. "Go on, then what happened?"

"So the girl looks up at me and says, 'I never been hit before. If you don't hit me hard, how am I going to know what it's like out in the street? Supposing I'm your partner out there on the street, what kind of a partner are you going to have if I don't know how to handle myself?' So, in a way, what she was saying to me was the same as when I was hitting on the sergeant."

He always liked to do the right thing. His motto was, "If a thing is worth doing, it's worth doing well," so it came as no surprise to Nanci when he graduated from the academy at the top of his class.

Now there was no getting away from it. She was married to a cop. A cop who was going to be a pilot, but a cop nevertheless.

But just a few weeks later, it took on a whole new meaning for her.

"Charlie's coming over for dinner tonight," she had told him when he walked in for dinner. "He called this morning. He's very excited. He's just bought a new house, he wants to tell us all about it. It seems like he's settling down. I'm so happy for him. And he wants to visit the baby. He hasn't seen Eric since he was born."

"Great," said Jimmy. "I can ask him about the accident I just heard about on the radio while I was driving home. It sounds pretty bad."

"What happened?" Nanci called from the kitchen.

"Two guys in the aviation unit doing a traffic survey over the Brooklyn Battery Tunnel were up in a helicopter. There was a plane ferrying people to New Jersey that was supposed to be flying over water to land near Battery Park. Only they took the shortcut and flew over land instead and the bottom of the plane hit the main rotor system of the blade of the helicopter. They both crashed. The plane landed in the water and the helicopter crew hit a building and they went down too."

Nanci said nothing. Of course, her first thought was to wonder if Charlie had been in that helicopter. But Jimmy didn't think like that, didn't live like that.

"When Charlie gets here, I'm hoping he can tell me more about it."

Charlie was late, so they started dinner without him. By this time Nanci had transmitted her growing anxiety to Jimmy.

When the phone rang, they both jumped. Nanci picked it up on her way into the kitchen.

"Jimmy, it's my father. He wants to speak to you."

Jimmy looked at her. He didn't move. "Your father wants to speak to me?"

"Yeah, come on, take it, he's waiting."

"I know what your father's going to say." And to her surprise Jimmy leaned over and buried his head in his hands. "It's him. I know it. If your dad wants to speak to me, that means Charlie was in that helicopter."

He got up and took the receiver from her. Seconds later he was holding out his arms to her and the tears were starting to roll down his face. She didn't need to ask, merely took the receiver from him, whispered a brief "We'll call you later, Dad," and took him in her arms.

They held each other for what seemed like an eternity, silently rocking back and forth in their grief.

But this was nothing to how they would feel at Charlie's funeral. He was given an inspector's funeral, just like all cops who died in the line of duty. Jimmy wore his uniform and the bagpipes played. Everybody had a lump in their throat when they saw Charlie's little brother walking behind the coffin, barely understanding what was happening. How would Eric feel if anything happened to Jason? Nanci wondered. Then Charlie's sister appeared and she bore an uncanny resemblance to her brother. More than anything, the sight of her face brought home to everyone the fact that they had lost Charlie.

"He once told me that if he died young, he wanted to go out with a big party," Jimmy whispered.

"He had his new house to move into, he had so much to look forward to. Why did he have to go now?" Nanci whispered back through her tears.

"You know, his father had this helicopter and that's why Charlie always wanted to fly. But you know what his father always said? 'Watch out when things are going too well.'"

That night Nanci lay awake and remembered Charlie and pondered about the enormity of the new career Jimmy was about to begin. Just as she had come to terms with the fact that his job would be safer than that of a cop on patrol, Charlie's tragic death brought home to her the dangers of Jimmy's work.

"That's crazy," Jimmy said. "There's nothing to worry about."

Jimmy was devastated by Charlie's death, but it didn't stop him wanting to fly. Nanci could see that he had taken to flying as easily as he had taken to everything else he had studied. That was the thing about Jimmy. Everything came easily to him. She watched him trying to help Jason with his math homework. The solution to any problem just leapt off the page at Jimmy, and he couldn't understand why Jason didn't get it.

But the flying was something else. He was working at Floyd Bennett Field, a big airfield in Brooklyn that had been used as a cargo stop in the Korean War and at the start of the Vietnam War. It was now the headquarters of the police department's special operations unit—immigration, emergency service, canine (bloodhounds, German shepherds). Every night Jimmy came home so excited, bursting to tell her all about it.

"They were going to put JFK there originally. They've got all these vehicles there, ERV's . . ."

"What's an ERV?" asked Nanci. Jimmy seemed to talk in initials these days.

"Emergency Response Vehicle. They got tanks they use for riots out there, armored vehicles where they took out the turret, the ones they use when they have to go into a place where people are shooting at them."

This is worse than the place where he helped make the A10 fighter planes, Nanci thought.

But then he made her laugh when he told her about Wrong Way Corrigan. That was the thing with Jimmy. He had the ability to amuse and charm her just when she needed it most.

"This guy called Corrigan took off from Floyd Bennett way back in 1938. He was supposed to be going to California but he landed up in Dublin, or maybe it was the other way around. His compass froze. He went the wrong way."

Jimmy had probably got it all wrong, but it was a good story and the way he acted it out made her and the boys laugh.

She was happy that Jimmy was happy despite her misgivings. Jimmy was often out on weekends doing work on people's planes so he could put in the hours to get his helicopter license. She remembered the veiled comments he had made when she had been going to her creative writing course on Saturdays, but she didn't say a word.

At night, when she couldn't get him to sleep, Nanci cradled baby Eric in her arms. Now Charlie would never see him. As she looked down at him, she thought about what someone had once said to her:

Sometimes when a life is taken, another is given.

They'd lost Charlie, but they had Eric.

And they also had Jason, and though Eric began to emerge as a sweet and loving little boy, Jason's old problems began to resurface.

They were calling her all the time from his school. Nanci thought back to the time, four years earlier, when she had had to face his horrible teacher in kindergarten.

"Jason is very intelligent"—this was the first thing the teacher always said—"but he just doesn't pay attention. He doesn't listen. He never sits still. He's always getting up from his seat and going over to throw stuff in the trash can when I'm talking. Or he'll drop his pencil on the floor. He's disrupting the other children. You have to do something."

I've heard this before, Nanci remembered. *Oh Lord, what do I do?* Jason had been at Montessori for a short time but they had had to take him out because it was too expensive. Now he was back in the public school system.

From what she could understand, the problem wasn't that he couldn't express himself. He was very articulate, *too* articulate, it seemed, because it got him in a lot of trouble at school. He appeared to be bored at school, but when he was at home, Nanci noticed that his homework seemed to go on for hours and hours. He wasn't just a typical sloppy, untidy little boy like all his friends. It was more than that. Jason was disorganized in a way that was beginning to alarm Nanci.

It wasn't that he was a loner child who sat in a room with books. His social skills were fine. If anything, Jason was a leader. He had loads of friends and they followed him around. But he didn't have Jimmy's quick instinctive grasp of things; he couldn't understand math and he didn't like sports and Jimmy didn't get it. Nanci was more sympathetic; where Jimmy had a hard time dealing with Jason, she was able to be more patient with him. She knew that she and Jimmy had to balance each other's strengths and weaknesses.

"Get him tested," they told her at the school. "See if there's anything wrong, let him have an IQ test."

His IQ was fine but his behavior wasn't.

"Well then, you should have his brain waves

tested. And you should take him to the school psychiatrist."

Nanci was searching. In a way, it was a relief to have something else on her mind besides her concern for Jimmy in the police force. She began to make regular visits to her local library. As often happened when she was seeking a solution to a problem, she came across it in a book. As she began to read about problems with children, she learned about something called attention deficit disorder.

She knew at once that this was what was wrong with Jason. Words like *disorganized, manic, hyper, creative, unpredictable, the highest IQ in the class, difficulty in paying attention, argue, postpone, procrastinate* leapt out at her from the page.

Suddenly she was aware of ADD everywhere she looked. She turned on the TV and there it was being discussed on *Good Morning America*. She picked up a magazine and there was an article on it.

But Jason's pediatrician looked at her and said, "No, no, no, Jason's not hyperactive. There's nothing wrong with him."

But Nanci knew that "hyperactive" was an

old-fashioned term for a real disorder that should not be dismissed.

"There *is* something wrong with him," Nanci pleaded. "Listen to me, *please*. Okay, sure, at home he can sit for hours on end doing a puzzle, but at school he can't sit still. Then again, sometimes at home we can all be playing a board game and suddenly he'll have the whole game on the floor. And he's different with each person. With some teachers he's okay and with others he's a nightmare."

Her worst problem, Nanci quickly came to realize, was that Jimmy had a hard time admitting anything was wrong. And even if he did acknowledge Jason had a problem, he didn't like putting a label on it. "What are you talking about? ADD, what is that? There's nothing wrong with Jason."

So it was going to be an uphill struggle. The difference between the two of them was that she felt driven to take further action, while Jimmy felt that loving Jason and taking care of him would be enough. Nanci knew she had to keep on at Jimmy until he understood they had to do something about Jason. Together.

"I've seen this flyer on the notice board at

the school about a parenting group," she said one night.

"A what? Group therapy? No way. Take Jason if you want."

"It's not about Jason, it's about us. It's to teach us how to be better parents. We can help Jason that way."

"I'm not going. There's nothing wrong with him. He'll do better if we don't make a huge deal out of everything."

"You promised you would always be a good father." She hated to manipulate him, but she was counting on the fact that Jimmy always had to do the right thing.

"Okay, I'll go. But only once. Just one time. But I want you to know, I think you're making a big thing of it."

Nanci wanted to jump for joy. Her determination had paid off. Now all she had to do was get him there. And she didn't have much time.

"So when is this parenting group?"

"It starts in half an hour. My mother's on her way over to watch the kids. Come on, Jimmy, get in the car."

She knew she had taken a big gamble, counting on the fact that she would be able to get Jimmy to go. But she had had to take that risk.

She was sad that they had come to this, but she knew it was for the best. They were still so young, not even thirty yet, and yet they were having to face pretty serious parental challenges. All around them, many of their friends were either still single with no responsibilities to tie them down or, if they were married, they had already given up and divorced. They seemed to be the only ones struggling with married life.

But if they could trade it in for a carefree life—no kids, no strings—Nanci knew she wouldn't even think twice about saying no thanks. She and Jimmy had made their choice and they were going to make it work.

NINE

🍑

When they walked into the counselors' office, two elderly women with gray hair introduced themselves. Connie and Ruth.

"They're lesbians," hissed Jimmy, and Nanci's heart sank.

She looked around the room. It was full of crystals and books, and she loved it, but she could sense that Jimmy was uncomfortable. He hadn't even taken off his coat.

Connie handed him a cup. "Have some green tea."

"*Green* tea?" Jimmy whispered to Nanci. "Who ever heard of green tea?"

"I'll have some, thanks," Nanci said quickly.

"Hi, how are you? Is this weird or what?" he

said to a man standing next to him who was looking even more uncomfortable than he was. Nanci was relieved to see that all the fathers looked as if they didn't want to be there. Maybe Jimmy sensed that too—that he was not alone—because he didn't leave.

There were no couches, just giant pillows on the floor, and everyone sat in a circle. Connie and Ruth asked each person to introduce themselves, and when it came to Jimmy's turn, he said, "My name is Jimmy and I don't want to be here."

Oh God, thought Nanci, *here we go.*

"But," Jimmy went on, "I'm not leaving. Now that I'm here, I'll stay. I told Nanci I didn't want to come and she told me I had to and so I told her I . . ."

That was the thing about Jimmy. He always said "I don't know what to say" and then he started talking and they couldn't get him to stop. She knew better than to smile, though, in case he saw her and thought she wasn't taking him seriously.

Connie and Ruth made everybody write down a secret they wanted to let go, but they didn't want anyone to know it was *their* secret. Connie collected everyone's secrets, mixed them all up, and read them out. When she came to one that read "I love to read pornography," she laughed and looked up.

"Who wrote that one?"

Everyone, including Jimmy, laughed with her, though of course no one admitted to it. The ice was broken.

In the end, they couldn't shut Jimmy up. Once he'd started talking, the inevitable happened. He would have been happy to sit there talking all night. He was so warm and open that she noticed everyone relaxing and coming out of their shells. He was always like that and it made her proud of him. He might not wholeheartedly approve of a situation, but he always made an effort to join in.

"So what did you think of them?" Nanci asked him on the way home.

"The Love Mothers?" he dubbed Connie and Ruth. It was a good name for them, Nanci thought. "They're not my bag but you know what? They're nice people. They're funny and they're wise. But I'm not going back. I told you. Only once."

Nanci sighed. He'd been once as he'd agreed. She couldn't expect any more from him.

But he surprised her. And it was the way he

always surprised her that constantly reaffirmed her love for him, Nanci thought. She had a feeling that he probably also surprised himself because he told her he'd learned something from Connie and Ruth.

"They're two loving people, that's what they are. They just want to help us through the crap in our lives, so we can be better parents. They want us to see that we can actually get by talking pleasant and nice to each other. You don't have to be angry. It's not necessary."

He'd always been angry, Nanci thought. He was nice and charming and anxious to do the right thing, but he could always get angry. It came from being a skinny little kid that other kids beat up on. He had to stand up for himself.

"You know, while we were all talking, I realized that I need to learn how to control my anger and channel it elsewhere. If I'm pissed off about something, I better wait until later to discuss the reason why, wait until I have calmed down."

Nanci was stunned to hear him talking like this. And thrilled.

They had gone to talk about Jason but, at Connie and Ruth's gentle instigation, they had wound up talking about themselves.

While Nanci was growing up, theirs was a neighborhood where, no matter how miserable you were, you never divorced. But now, all around them, their friends and relatives were getting divorced.

Somehow, Nanci always thought, she and Jimmy were different from other couples. They often went out to dinner with married friends who argued all the time. Their old friend Joe had split up with his wife, Misty. Now Nanci was confronted with the first divorce in her own family. Her sister Linda, who was a spitfire, and hilarious to boot, was splitting from her husband.

The irony was that everyone had had a big wedding except Nanci and Jimmy. All the couples who were splitting up all around them had had engagement rings, engagement parties, receptions, bridesmaids, honeymoons in Hawaii, the whole nine yards, and she had had nothing but a dress and a bouquet of flowers to hold over her protruding stomach.

In spite of that, they seemed to live a charmed life somehow. But now Nanci realized their problems were serious.

"Fighting is okay," Connie and Ruth had told them. *We don't fight*, Nanci was about to say but then she realized that they did. They argued about all sorts of things, about Jason, about Jimmy's habit of always telling her how his mother did things.

"You have to learn to argue, that's okay, but you don't have to become enemies," they were told. "You can disagree and still be on the same side. And you have to leave your parents out of it. Your marriage is not about your parents' marriage. You came from their families, but now you are your own family, and you need to focus on that. Find time for yourselves. It's okay to have separate interests; that's not going to tear you apart. That's what makes your relationship interesting. Nanci doesn't have to play hockey, and Jimmy, you don't have to read poetry. You can go to poetry readings and she can go to hockey games—or not. What's important is that you both get to do the things you want and also find time to be together."

It was good advice, and it helped. But they both knew that keeping a love alive in spite of life's pressures sometimes called for bigger actions.

Nanci could not forget the magical time they had spent on Long Island.

But now Jimmy's parents had retired to the house. Nanci and Jimmy could not afford a house of their own out there, so it would mean living with his parents again until they had saved enough money to buy their own home. His parents were willing and Jimmy was prepared to commute.

"I could do it. Maybe your parents would let me stay with them in the middle of the week, then I would only have to drive out twice a week. The boys could be raised by the sea; they could have the childhood I had in the summers. It would be a better thing for all of us."

Especially Jason, thought Nanci. If we can get him away to the fresh air and the ocean, things will be better.

It was a big decision but gradually it all came together. Jason was eleven and Eric was five. They would both benefit so much from a childhood in the outdoors, close to the beach. Nanci could not believe that at last they were taking steps to make their dream come true. Soon they would be leaving the dirt and grime of Brooklyn behind them to start a new life at the beach.

She had no idea that with the move to Long Island, their real troubles were about to begin.

TEN

❧

"We're going out to get ice cream," Nanci called to Jimmy's parents as they went out the door. She heard her mother-in-law laugh.

By now the words "Going to get ice cream" were a family joke.

"We're not fooling anyone," she said to Jimmy as they drove away in the van.

"Especially when we come home without the ice cream," Jimmy said, laughing. He drove the van along deserted roads, past a large pond and an osprey nest balanced precariously on a tall pole. He swung the van down the road where Nanci had had her cottage during the Summer of Love, and parked on the bay.

He turned and took her in his arms. Within

seconds their kissing had taken on a frantic intensity. Nanci's blouse was already undone as they climbed over the seats into the back of the van and stretched out on the pile of blankets to make love.

As soon as they had made the move out to Long Island, it was as if she had gone back ten years in time. Once again they were living with her in-laws and privacy was a thing of the past. Any sound echoed throughout the house, so she and Jimmy had taken to escaping in their van whenever they wanted to make love. In the summer, they found a deserted spot on the beach, or sometimes they were very creative and took the boat out into the middle of the bay. And in winter they used the back of the van.

And if Nanci had thought they would find peace and quiet there, she was mistaken. Her in-laws' living room had a mass of furniture in it, two huge recliners, a couch, a chair, a table, and a bank of VCR tapes. The TV was on twenty-four hours a day. His work as a transit cop down in the subways had impaired Jimmy's father's hearing, so the TV was always turned up full blast. *Wheel of Fortune, Jeopardy, Golden Girls,* the Weather Channel.

Now Jimmy had a two-and-a-half-hour commute to work, so he had to leave the house at 4:30 A.M. During the week he stayed with her parents. Nanci never complained about the lack of privacy, because she could appreciate all the hours Jimmy was putting into his work. And she could see that he loved helicopter flying. When he came back on the weekend, he was full of stories about dropping scuba divers into the Hudson River to rescue someone who had jumped off a bridge, or hoisting people out of the water when a boat had overturned. And all the time he was off on trips to Texas to be upgraded on the latest pilot training, mechanical systems, and emergency procedures with helicopters.

Living at such close quarters would never have worked if Nanci's in-laws had not been such a wonderful couple. Harold, Jimmy's father, was always inviting her to "come over and sit down, chew the fat with me." He made great conversation and he had the gift of making anyone feel at home. And her mother-in-law was such an easygoing person. She had been a working woman and she was warm and insightful about the problems a wife and mother had to face.

But what really brought home to Nanci how close she and her mother-in-law had become was when she discovered how easy it was to share a kitchen with her. And it was a tiny kitchen. With two women in there preparing their family's meals, it became very crowded, but not once did Barbara Jean make Nanci feel unwelcome. On the contrary, it was in the kitchen that her mother-in-law fed Nanci much-needed words of encouragement. Now they were all living under one roof, Barbara Jean could see the problems Nanci was having with Jason—and with Jimmy.

"Don't keep it locked in," she told Nanci. "I can see it drives you crazy the way Jimmy gets angry about Jason. His telling Jason to 'shape up' all the time isn't going to work."

Nanci nodded, encouraging her mother-in-law to talk.

"Jimmy's always been angry," Barbara Jean said. "He gets it from his father. My sons are great guys to hang out with, but somehow there was a lot of anger created while they were growing up. Jimmy's father is a sweetheart, but he had a temper. I remember one time when Jimmy was a kid, he mouthed off at him and Harry grabbed the first thing that came to hand and went after him. It was a hatchet. He never caught Jimmy but I saw all that rage—I often wonder what I would have done if he had caught him."

Nanci couldn't help wondering what it had done to Jimmy, being chased like that by his father—even if he knew it was a brief moment of rage from an otherwise loving man. "But you love Harry?" Nanci asked.

"Of course I love him. I never stopped loving him. You love Jimmy no matter how clumsy he can be. In a marriage, you have to give each other leeway on your flaws. Don't forget, we have our flaws too."

In 1989, a year after they moved out to Long Island, another part of their dream came true. They got a lucky break: their name came up in the lottery for affordable housing, and they moved into their own home.

It wasn't on the water, but it was a perfect spot. Tucked away on a little road in the middle of the woods, their new home had a big yard, a wraparound porch, and a wonderful design for the ground floor where the living room, the den, the kitchen, and the hall all ran into one another, creating a close family unit for them to share. Upstairs there were four bedrooms.

As they settled in and grew used to their new home, Nanci held her breath. Maybe now they were on track for the future.

But there was still one big pressure on their happiness.

Jason.

Nanci had to face facts. They'd now been out on Long Island for three years. Jason was fourteen. By now he was in East Hampton Middle School, but it was the same old story. *Can you come up to the school, we've put him in detention, we've put him in special ed, he's very smart but he doesn't listen.* . . . Nanci knew that some mothers would be defensive and argue and say, "That can't possibly be my son, he's not like that," but she couldn't say that because she knew it wasn't true. Jason *was* like that and he was getting worse. It didn't help that Jimmy was away so much. Jason needed his father. Nanci found she was becoming too exhausted to deal with him on her own.

Yet she had to find the strength somewhere. He was her Jason, and she loved him for the very things that made him so difficult to be around sometimes: his passion, his individuality, his creativity. Much of the time she identified with him, his determination to be independent. She wished she could get closer to him. Eric was an easygoing little boy who was happy to be held. But Jason kept his distance. She could feel the sensitive little child locked inside an older boy's body. She missed that little boy. When she looked at this angry teenager, she felt his pain.

They put him in a special class. They called it "alternative" but Nanci knew it was really about getting kids like Jason away from the others and isolating them. In a way it was a good thing, because there were only ten kids in the class, but on the other hand, Nanci reflected, it was ten kids with problems. Some of them were very slow and learning disabled, which had never been Jason's challenge.

But Jason surprised them. He told Nanci, "I'm going to show them I don't belong there," and he worked himself out of it, controlling himself, managing to avoid fights. Nanci was so proud of him. Pretty soon he was back in the regular school. But he still couldn't pay attention. He was incredibly disorganized. He carried his backpack full of books weighing fifty pounds around with him all day because he could never remember to leave time to go pick them up from his locker. If they were on his back, at least he knew he had them.

Nanci's heart broke for him when she saw him with that huge backpack. Like Jimmy, he wanted to do the right thing and got angry with himself when he couldn't. And Jimmy's hands were tied. He'd accepted the long commute and separation from the family because they had agreed that the family would be better out of the city. But he knew that Jason needed him to be there.

They were all so frustrated, each struggling, each trying to do their best, but it just never seemed to be enough. Jimmy and Jason would bury their frustration except when it burst out into anger. And it was getting to the stage where Eric was getting upset and starting to cry; she would have to send him to the neighbor to get him away from all the tension. And then Jason would walk out the door and she would call Jimmy again in tears. She needed her husband's strength to help her control Jason.

"Tell him to stop it at once," Jimmy yelled over the phone.

"Jimmy, he's walking down the highway with his backpack, running away from home. You want me to run after him and pick him up and put him over my shoulder and send him to his room with no dinner? Get real!"

One day about a year later, when Nanci was picking Eric up from school, one of his former teachers approached her.

"Hi, remember me? I'm Suzanne. Tell me, how is Jason?"

"He's in the tenth grade and he's having a very hard time, as you probably know."

"That's why I'm asking," Suzanne said. "I have a son who is a year older, and you know, my son has attention deficit disorder. I just found out about it. You know what it is, don't you?"

"I do. I read about it some time ago," Nanci said. "I guess you're asking how Jason is because you're thinking what I've been thinking for a long time. I thought he had ADD but my pediatrician told me back then that he didn't have it."

"They said the same about my boy," Suzanne said, "but I didn't believe them and I started going to these support groups. Why don't you come along? My son has just been diagnosed and now he takes Ritalin. I can't tell you what a difference it makes. It used to be like it was the Antichrist coming through the door when he got home from school. Sometimes it was really off-the-wall behavior and I was scared."

Nanci thought about what Suzanne had said. Jason was getting worse. What really frightened her was the way she was beginning to feel. *I love him,* she thought, *but I can't take it anymore.* She just didn't know what to think from day to day. He was always funny, but he had a bad temper and he could argue with the Pope. He was relentless, he kept on coming at her, wearing her down, exhausting her, and more than once she had had her hand on a saucepan ready to hurl it at him.

At that point she always had to walk away. Because Jason never walked away. Nanci knew she was on her own in a potentially violent situation with her own son. She could see little Eric was totally confused. He adored his older brother but he received constant abuse from him and he didn't understand why.

The more she thought about it, the more she knew she had to go with Suzanne.

When she walked into the cafeteria in the huge high school up island she was not prepared for the sight that greeted her. There were at least two hundred people in the room. There were loudspeakers, there were tables piled high with information pamphlets, and there was a doctor saying the very words she wanted to hear.

"Here's a picture of the brain. ADD *does* exist. It's not something that somebody made up. Millions of Americans have it today and most of them do not even know that they have it. It is not a learning disability; it has nothing to do with low intelligence."

All the people in the room had children like the ones he described, and for the first time in a long while Nanci knew she wasn't alone. *I'm not crazy*, she thought.

Jason was diagnosed. Ritalin was prescribed. Jason had to take a dose in the morning and then he had to remember to go and see the nurse at school and get another dose at lunchtime.

But just when Nanci was feeling relief that she'd found help for Jason, things took another wrong turn.

* * *

Jason was fine with the Ritalin. Too fine. He liked the way it made him feel and he started taking more than he was supposed to.

And just as Nanci was beginning to suspect what was happening, Jason introduced two new friends to her.

One was Suzanne's son and the other was named Jack. Nanci especially adored Jack, who was sweet and mannerly.

"Why haven't I ever met him before?" she asked Jason.

"Oh, he's from Montauk. He's been in rehab."

Rehab!

Nanci calmed herself down. She knew Jack had taken drugs but he was straight now. It was only natural that Jason should hang with another kid who'd had problems, she thought.

But after a while she noticed Jack was no longer around. When she asked Jason about him, he said casually, "Oh, he's back in rehab."

"He was doing drugs again?"

Jason nodded. She expected him to tell her to back off, to tell her to leave his friends alone. But he didn't leave the room. He was pacing up and down in front of her, but he wasn't going anywhere.

"What kind of drugs?" She tried to sound nonchalant. She didn't want Jason to see how upset she was. Inside she was screaming, *Have you been doing drugs? Please Jason, tell me you have not been doing drugs.* "I'm only asking because I was wondering what kind of drugs kids do these days. Do they smoke pot still?"

"Well, Jack was doing a little LSD."

"LSD? I thought that was a sixties kind of a thing. What else do they do?"

"Inhale stuff."

"Like what?"

"Paint thinner, butane fuel. Bathroom sprays, anything that gets you high."

Nanci took a deep breath. Jason was fifteen years old. Jack was sixteen.

"Jason, were you doing all these things with Jack?"

He stopped pacing, stood squarely in front of her.

Oh my God, she thought, *he's going to hit me.*

"Yeah."

"You know, inhaling things, it's more than smoking a joint. That stuff is going straight to your brain. Are you trying to kill yourself?"

"I don't know."

"Jason, tell me, do you think you might have a problem?"

"I think I might." He was looking straight at her now and she saw with horror the tears beginning to well up in his eyes.

"Jason," she said as gently as she could, "you're taking Ritalin, you're doing LSD, you're inhaling paint thinner. It seems to me that you are doing more than trying to get high. You're trying to do yourself serious harm. Why is that? Are you that sad? What can we do to help?"

He was sobbing now. Her great big son who had come close to terrorizing her so recently was crying in her arms as if he were the little black-haired baby in her dream all those years ago.

"I want you to help me, Mom. I've wanted help for so long. Please, Mom, do something for me. I'm so scared."

"Jason, of course I'll help you. It's all I've ever wanted to do for years and years. Maybe you need to go into rehab too."

She heard him say "Yes" as he sobbed on her shoulder.

* * *

Nanci called Barbara Jean and told her what had happened. "I'm going to have to tell Jimmy tonight," Nanci said, "and I think it would be better if Jason wasn't here."

"Bring him straight here," Barbara Jean said.

She drove Jason over to Lazy Point and went home, got Eric to bed, and sat down to wait for Jimmy.

When he walked through the door, she said straight away, "We need to talk."

Immediately he asked, "Where's Jason?"

"He's not here right now. He's at your parents', he's okay, but we've got big problems. He's been doing drugs. With his friend Jack. Jack is in rehab and Jason has admitted that he needs help."

Jimmy sat down and wept.

Nanci broke down and cried along with him. They were releasing months of pent-up worry about Jason.

Once Jimmy was through crying, he got angry.

"I want to help our son," Nanci heard him say. He had his head in his hands and he was shaking. "But I don't know how. All this time you've been trying to tell me he had a big problem, and I never listened like I should have. I think I knew deep down but I didn't want to face it. Oh, Nanci, what are we going to do? I don't understand problems like this one. I worry about stuff like when we can't pay a bill and I have to find the money or I want to stay out here with you and they call me into work for another tour. But how to help Jason—that's got me beat. And it makes me so angry. Do you have any idea how frustrated I feel? I'm his dad, for God's sake, and I can't do anything."

"I know." Nanci put her arm around him and rested her head on his shoulder. They sat side by side at the kitchen table, feeling more helpless than at any other time in their marriage.

She understood Jimmy's despair. She knew he loved Jason, but he had never been able to identify with his eldest son in quite the same way she had. She knew she had to be there for both of them during the coming months.

But nothing could have prepared her for the way Jimmy's sadness manifested itself. His pain was raw and constantly visible and she ached for him. But he dealt with it in the worst possible way. Instead of sharing it with Nanci, he began to withdraw from her emotionally, to disappear into a place inside himself just when she needed him most.

And as she reached out for him, desperately wanting to help him, he was no longer there.

ELEVEN

❦

How can *I help him*, Nanci kept asking herself, *when he's never here?*

To her horror, Jimmy avoided the turmoil at home by taking on more and more work. But he was in denial, and refused to see that that was what he was doing.

"Nanci, I'm working twenty hours a day. I'm doing forty-two and a half hours a week on the police job and then I'm working another thirty or forty on another job so we can afford to live out here. I'm traveling back and forth in the car another fifteen hours a week. All I got left is time to sleep. And we both agree that I'm terrible with Jason. Maybe it's better if I stay away."

"No, Jimmy, you're wrong," she pleaded.

"He needs you. We both need you. We have a crisis here. Please be here to help me with it."

But the more she appealed to him, the more he backed away. And what made it even worse was that in a way she could sympathize with his urge to run away from it all.

And it wasn't as if he was just working two hours away in Brooklyn. Now he was going to Texas on a regular basis for the upgrading courses he was required to take as a helicopter pilot. Nanci found herself coming home from work and sitting down on her bed and crying. She read a novel in which she came across a line that said something like "It's always harder to be left than to do the leaving." That was exactly right. And she felt Jimmy was always leaving them. She often found things in books that she could identify with. When she had read *The Awakening* by Kate Chopin, she had come across the term *mother-woman*, someone who "idolized her children and worshipped her husband and esteemed it a holy privilege to efface herself as an individual." Nanci knew she could never be a mother-woman. She was a woman first, and a mother and a wife second. Now she was a woman who was being left all the time. She missed Jimmy so much, but at the same time she couldn't help feeling angry that she was having to deal with Jason on her own.

But when they finally got Jason into rehab, an hour and a half up the island, she felt a huge sense of achievement.

And even better, she began to have hope that things would be better from now on.

Jimmy went with her to take Jason to Apple, the rehab center. Jason would be there for eighteen months. He would go to school there and it would be the best thing in the world that could happen to him in the worst possible way. It was what he needed so desperately, Nanci thought. She was only sorry he had to go through it at all.

For the first month they weren't allowed to see him at all, but after that they were allowed to visit.

And with Jason gone, a new calm settled over the house. Eric missed his brother but at the same time, Nanci saw, he could come out of his shell. He didn't have to be afraid of Jason anymore, and he could look forward to the time when Jason came home and he could love him again.

This period of calm should have been the

end of their nightmares, the time when she and Jimmy had a chance to talk things through and rediscover the love they both knew was still there.

And maybe it would have been if Nanci hadn't met The Women.

*S*he was cleaning the house one morning when there was a knock on the door.

The woman who stood there wore jeans and a sweatshirt and had short red hair. She was carrying coffee and a bagel, which she held out to Nanci.

"I brought these for you," she said.

"Do I know you?" Nanci was amazed. But she couldn't help smiling. The woman seemed so warm and friendly.

"No, but I thought it was time you did. Our sons are friends. My name is Luanne and I'm Jack's mother. We've spoken on the phone. Here, I've brought you breakfast, can I come in?"

"Sure." Nanci held open the door.

"I'm here because I know what you're going through and I want to help. I know what it's like. This is Jack's second bout with rehab. One day they're here and in your face and the next day they're not and you're left with all these emotions. So I thought it might help if we got to know each other."

Nanci liked her immediately. Luanne was the outgoing, take-charge kind of woman that Nanci needed in her life. Nanci was strong. She knew what she had to do to get through having a son in rehab, but as they talked, she realized that this woman had twice as much experience and she was offering exactly the kind of support Nanci needed—but wasn't getting—from Jimmy.

"I am so happy to meet you," she told Luanne. "We came out here so Jason wouldn't be anywhere near things like drugs and gangs in the city, and look what happens. There are four kids all in rehab from the same school. And the school is like, 'Good riddance, they're gone, no one else does drugs.' And it's not true. We were just the lucky ones who were able to get help. Something ought to be done."

"I agree," Luanne, said. "We should start a group or something. Come for coffee tomorrow and meet another mom with a teenage son our boys' age."

The other woman, Molly, was Irish. Not American Irish but someone who had been born in Ireland and still had the brogue. Nanci had always felt an affinity with the Irish from the days she spent with her Swedish-Irish grandmother in Vermont.

It wasn't deliberate on her part. Nanci wasn't actively seeking new women friends. She had plenty of confidantes. She had her mother-in-law. She hadn't gone out and drawn these women into her life. They had found her. And the reason that they very quickly became close was because despite the fact that they were totally different, they had something in common—they were all mothers of adolescent sons—and this united them in such a close bond that it could not compare with Nanci's other female friendships.

But there was something else that drew Nanci to Molly and Luanne.

All her life, Nanci had wanted to be independent, to have control over her own life. And her new friends seemed to personify the kind of woman she had always hoped to become.

She admired their strength and their confidence.

She wanted to be like them and she was flattered that they seemed happy to include her in their lives.

One morning they turned up with a surprise.

"We've got a proposition for you, Nanci."

Nanci was intrigued. Knowing these two, it could be anything.

"We know your work at the restaurant came to an end last week." This was true. Nanci had been waitressing at a café in East Hampton, but she had only been hired for a few weeks. "So we were wondering if you would like to join us in our work. We clean houses and we have a lot of fun. We figure the more the merrier. We'd get the work done faster and keep each other company as we worked."

"Sure," said Nanci, "that'd be great. I know how to clean. I used to be a chambermaid at a motel." It wasn't ideal work, but if they all had the right attitude toward it, they could make it worthwhile.

So they began to work together during the day and in the evenings they discussed what they could do to make people aware that there were kids who had drug problems in East Hampton. They came up with an acronym for what they would call their support group. CHANGE. Community Helping A New Generation Evolve.

The CHANGE meetings took place at her

house, and suddenly Nanci found her home filled with people with whom she could identify, telling their stories, reaching out for help. One woman spoke of how her son had ended up killing himself. She told them how lucky they were that Jason and the other kids were in rehab. It was the best thing. Her words showed Nanci that she and Jimmy were being given a chance to rescue their son's life, a chance that this poor woman had never had.

Eventually, when the house became too crowded, they rented a church basement and invited as many people as they could think of. They had to make people interested in their cause. On the first night they got a terrific turnout, so for the next meeting they hired a speaker, just as Nanci had seen when she went to the ADD support group with Suzanne.

But only six people showed up. The consensus was, *other people* had a problem with *their* kids but it didn't affect anybody else. There was no problem at the high school. These people were ostriches, Nanci thought. She wrote letters to the local paper, venting her frustration.

So it was that over the coming months Nanci found herself seeing far more of Molly and Luanne than she saw of Jimmy. She didn't plan it.

In fact she didn't even notice it until one night a conversation with Jimmy brought everything to a head.

It was a beautiful summer day, and as they had finished cleaning early, she and Molly and Luanne took off for the beach.

She came home from the beach to find him standing in the kitchen with a glass of vodka in his hand.

"You're home?" she said, surprised. "When did you get home?"

"About half an hour ago. I've been calling you all day."

"I've been at the beach. How was your day?"

"With The Women?"

"Who?"

"Molly and Luanne?"

She didn't like the way he said their names, and she didn't like the look of his ugly mood.

"Yes, with Molly and Luanne," she said slowly.

"While I've been sitting in a car in ninety-degree heat wearing a suit and tie all day, you've been relaxing at the beach?"

She didn't say anything. On top of everything else, when things had been really bad with Jason, Jimmy had taken on security work. This habit of moonlighting, of working two or three jobs, was something many cops did. Jimmy's father had always taken on extra work, and it seemed to be something Jimmy took for granted. It had started when they needed the money, and it had escalated when Jimmy had wanted to escape from the problems with Jason.

His current security job was watching the four-year-old daughter of a Hamptons millionaire to see nobody kidnapped her. Jimmy was an action man. To sit in a parked car on a hot Saturday afternoon watching a kid was his idea of hell. In fact, Nanci could see it would be anybody's idea of hell. He took *Reader's Digest* and crossword puzzles, but even so the time passed very slowly. He had to take the kid and her nanny to the movies and sit in the back row of a movie theater watching *Bambi,* and he felt like an idiot because he had to wear a security uniform and everyone stared at him. Nanci hated to see him put in such an uncomfortable position.

Yet something told her that this was about something else.

He went on, "You go to the beach. Do you

know how that makes me feel? Do you have any idea what a terrific life you have, Nanci, staying at home, taking care of the kids, going off to the beach whenever you feel like it?"

"Jimmy," she said carefully, "if it'll make you feel better, I'll work more, I'll work weekends too. *You* stay home."

"Oh, yeah, sure. You only make ten dollars an hour."

"It's not about the money," she said as patiently as she could. "The point is not how much money you're making but that you're never here and that doesn't work for either of us. What are you working for? Just for the money? It's supposed to be for me and the boys, but you never see us. At least if I took up some of the slack, you would be home and we'd see each other occasionally."

"If you worked weekends, would it be with The Women?"

So that was what this was about. He resented her spending time with Molly and Luanne.

"Jimmy, I work with these people but it's not just that. Their support about Jason is invaluable."

"But you never do anything with me anymore," he said, raising his eyes to meet hers in an almost childlike plea. "We have nothing in common anymore. You don't come to hockey with me."

"Oh, Jimmy, that's crazy," she said, laughing, trying to shake him out of his mood. "You never asked me to."

But he began to reel off a list of things they never did together anymore, and as she looked at him, she recalled something he had said when they were out having dinner with friends.

"Well, I'm glad to hear you two are having fun," he'd said to them. "I don't know what that's like anymore. Nanci won't come flying with me, she won't do anything with me. She's too busy."

She had turned to him in astonishment. "But Jimmy, you never asked me to go flying with you. Am I supposed to guess that's what you want to do?"

He was hurt, she realized, he was lonely. And he had been trying to tell her what he was feeling through other people.

But part of the problem was that they were always *with* other people. Jimmy had this weird habit of always asking other people along so they would never be alone. She could never pin him down. She would say, "Did you invite these people or not? What are you telling me? Will we be alone or not?"

And he would answer, "Oh, you know, they might show up." He would never give her a straight answer and it would drive her crazy.

"Jimmy, *did* you invite them?" she'd ask. "Because if you invited them, they're going to show up and we're not going to be on our own."

And he'd say, "Oh, I don't know, I might have mentioned that we'd see them at one o'-clock at the airport."

"Well then, they'll show up," she'd sigh. "We *are* going with them. We're not doing something on our own like you said you wanted. So why don't you go with them, because I'm not interested anymore."

Nanci didn't like being like this but he drove her to it. And then he had the nerve to tell the same people when they saw them at dinner, "Nanci won't go sailing with me, Nanci won't go flying with me."

And then people started saying things to her like "Nanci, when do you ever see your husband? I bet you never see him, because he's at the baseball field all the time, he's at the hockey rink all the time. When is he ever home? You poor thing, you must miss him." These remarks made her face the truth: He was spending time away from home because he did not want to be there. She had been trying to convince herself that she was crazy to think that there was anything seriously wrong between them. But the fact that other people were beginning to notice made it legitimate.

She couldn't ignore it any longer.

The marriage was in real trouble.

TWELVE

Six months later things were even worse.

For the first time since she had been married to Jimmy, Nanci was keeping something from him.

She was planning a trip to Ireland with Molly and Luanne, and she hadn't said a word to Jimmy. She felt bad about it but she felt even worse about the fact that they seemed to be drifting apart. She was unhappy. And she could tell he was unhappy. Yet neither of them seemed to be able to do anything about it.

Nanci knew that Jimmy did not share her excitement about her new female friends. It wasn't that he didn't like them, more that he felt left out.

Sometimes Nanci felt torn between her new friends and Jimmy.

"Guess who's calling again," Molly asked.

Nanci knew it was Jimmy. It seemed as if he called half a dozen times a day, and Nanci wondered if he genuinely missed her or if he was checking up on her.

Then, right before she left for Ireland, they had a serious argument. It was only a few days before she was due to leave and Nanci still hadn't told him. She kept putting it off. Nanci had invited her sister and brother-in-law to stay for the weekend. She figured that if she told Jimmy about Ireland when they were there, he wouldn't do anything in front of them. She knew it was cowardly and unfair, but she was desperate to go on this trip.

After dinner they sat around the fire reading the Sunday *New York Times*. Nanci had been going to night school with Molly, taking a course in travel and tourism, and of course this was another thorn in Jimmy's side. She had grown accustomed to reading the Travel section of the *Times* and she was studying it now, searching for something about Ireland.

Suddenly Jimmy plucked the paper out of

her hand, crumpled it up, and threw it on the fire.

"All you do is read," he said.

For a second Nanci was in shock. This was so totally unlike Jimmy. He was never rude or ill mannered in this way. He had a temper, sure, but he never lost control like this in front of other people. He must be in a worse state than she realized, Nanci thought.

"Why did you do that?" she cried.

"Like I said, all you do is read," Jimmy repeated and laughed, trying to make a joke out of it.

Nanci's brother-in-law laughed with him. Nanci looked at her sister. The two men thought it was all so funny and it was awful. But Nanci would not fight in public. She let it go. Jimmy was trying to tell her something, but why couldn't he come out and say to her? Like, "Nanci, please could you take time out from your reading so we can spend some time together? Would you spend the evening talking to me instead of reading?"

If he had told her gently what was bothering him instead of throwing her newspaper on the fire, then of course she would have under-

stood, Nanci thought. And on top of everything, she had to tell him she had been keeping
something from him.

She told him that night.

"You are not going," he said immediately.

It was a throwback to her father, Nanci
thought, telling her what she could and
couldn't do.

"Yes, I am. I'm paying for the trip. I'm not
asking you for a thing. I've worked and I've
saved the money for it. You don't understand
about Molly and Luanne because you don't
have any close friends like I do. You have the
guys you work with, but they're not real
friends, they don't support you like Molly and
Luanne do."

"Oh, yes they do," he yelled at her suddenly,
and she listened in horror as all his frustration
of the last few months came bubbling to the
surface. "They've been telling me I should get
out and have fun with them. They've been
telling me I'm too good to you. I put up with
too much. Yeah, okay, you're right, I resent the
time and the attention you give to these
women. I think you should be spending time
with me."

"Well, I resent the time you spend working and helping out other people. I'm going to Ireland. It's a dream I've always had and I'm going to make it come true."

Even as she said the words, she thought about their dream. They'd got away from Brooklyn, they lived by the sea, but where had it got them?

To the point where they could barely communicate anymore.

Molly was from County Clare, so after they landed at Shannon Airport, they went straight there. They didn't have an agenda. When they couldn't stay with Molly's relatives, they'd stay in B&B's.

It was everything that Nanci had dreamt it would be. The warmth with which she was greeted by Molly's brothers and sisters and cousins was especially welcome after her frosty parting from Jimmy. There was a lot of drinking and merriment, and Nanci found she was spending most of her time in pubs, singing. Molly's husband Sean had played in bands all over Ireland, and everywhere they went, people knew him. Out came the fiddles and everyone wanted to sing a song for the wife of their old friend. Nanci couldn't remember when she had had so much fun.

So when she met Tommy O'Reilly in a pub in Limerick one night, she was in a happy and relaxed frame of mind. Her skin was glowing in the firelight and her dark eyes shone with excitement.

From the minute they had set foot on Irish soil, Nanci had felt at home and Molly had been determined to introduce her to as many people as possible.

Tommy O'Reilly was tall, much taller than Jimmy. He wasn't as good-looking as her husband, Nanci thought, but he had a twinkle in his eye. He had been a musician with Molly's husband. Nanci saw immediately that he had the very qualities that had always attracted her to Jimmy. He was outgoing and charming, full of the blarney.

Molly teased him, "I can see you've got your eye on Nanci, Tommy. I'll tell you something, she's keen to take a walk on the moors."

"Is she now?" Tommy said, eyeing Nanci, who blushed.

"I do want to take a walk on the moors," she

said to Tommy, her face serious, "but I mean a walk. There's a difference."

They went up to the moors the next day and it was beautiful and green. If it had been a bit warmer, Nanci would have kicked off her shoes and run over the hills like Julie Andrews in *The Sound of Music*.

Then he took her to an old hotel that was like something out of a movie, all misty and magical. There was a big hall filled with people having tea and sandwiches, a family gathered to plan their wedding, priests visiting with their mothers. Tommy went straight to the piano and to Nanci's delight he began singing raucous Bette Midler songs. He had a low raspy voice and Nanci stood up beside the piano to sing along with him. They didn't notice his cigarette fall into the piano and suddenly smoke filled the air. They'd set the piano on fire.

"Quick!" yelled Tommy, taking her by the hand. "We're out of here." And they ran through the hall and into the grounds. Still holding her hand, he looked deep into her eyes.

"I think you're beautiful," Tommy told her. "I wish you'd leave your husband and stay in Ireland with me."

She laughed. She liked this man. He was quite a character, and wherever they went, if there was a piano in the pub, he sat down and played and started singing. Nanci was enjoying herself. She didn't feel threatened by him but she was lapping up the attention.

One day he took them to a pool hall. It was in the village where he had grown up; he was staying in a hotel there because his mother had died and the family house had been sold. Molly went off to visit some friends and Tommy announced he was going back to the hotel to change for the evening.

"Molly's not back, so why don't you come with me?" he said to Nanci.

In his hotel room he pushed her gently against the door and kissed her.

"You're so beautiful," he told her, as indeed he told her every day.

Nanci didn't fight him off. She wasn't physically attracted to him but it was nice to have someone show they liked her. It was just as well he wasn't more good-looking, she thought, because then she might have been tempted to take it a bit further. As it was, nothing happened.

And then when Tommy understood that he

wasn't going to get any further with her, he moved on from Nanci to one of the beautiful Fitzgerald sisters they met in a pub one night.

"Didn't I tell you?" Molly said. "He's full of shite."

She said goodbye to him and never heard from him again. But her brief time spent with Tommy had woken her up to the fact that she desperately missed the affection and attention she'd once had from Jimmy.

THIRTEEN

❦

*N*anci had to admit that for a short while, the trip to Ireland did her marriage a lot of good.

Jimmy's welcome home was touching. He had filled the house with cut flowers, and their scent wafted through the rooms. The night she came in from the airport, he arranged for Eric to spend a couple hours at a friend's house, and when she walked into the house, she was greeted by the sight of the table laid for a candlelit dinner.

It was Chinese takeout but what the heck? He had made an effort, he was trying to tell her something, and it touched her.

"I'm glad to have you home," he said simply, pouring her a glass of her favorite chardonnay. "I've missed you. I didn't know it was possible to miss you so much. Every night you've been gone, I've lain in our bed upstairs wanting you. Look at the bags under my eyes. You did that, Nanci. I couldn't sleep without you."

"Oh, what are you talking about?" She laughed, leaned over and kissed him. "You sleep at my mom's two nights a week, and she tells me you snore away quite happily there."

"You know what I mean." He was serious. "And if you don't believe me, I'll show you later."

Later that night as she lay in his arms, she was about to tell him about Tommy in Ireland. But then he said something so beautiful that she knew she couldn't spoil the moment.

"Nanci," he whispered, "the truth is that even though we may have had some problems in our marriage, whenever we're in bed together, we never just have sex—we always make love. I love you, Nanci."

"I love you too," she told him, "more than ever."

And the following week, when they went to pick up Jason from rehab and bring him home forever, Nanci knew that now everything was going to be all right.

She was wrong.

Within two years they were back to where they had been before Nanci went to Ireland.

She tried to figure out how it had happened, and finally felt it wasn't her fault—or Jimmy's. If anything, his work was to blame. Once again Jimmy had slipped into the old pattern of taking on too much extra work. They needed the money. Jason would be going to college soon. And Jimmy had to go the twenty-year distance on the force to get his pension. But Nanci couldn't help feeling that working among all those disillusioned "lost souls," as Jimmy called them—the hard-line cops who were divorced, had become alcoholics, were just marking time till they could get out—some of their influence had to rub off on him.

They were drifting again and this time Nanci wasn't sure she had the energy to get everything back on track.

"Oh, there they go, the witches, they're at it again."

It was a cold winter evening in 1995, Nanci

and her sister Joie were curled up by the fire, and Jimmy kept wandering in and out, listening to their conversation. Then he would turn around and go back to watching the game on TV in the other room. He always did this when Joie came out from the city to stay for the weekend. He was half kidding, he didn't really think they were witches, but at the same time he didn't understand what the heck they were talking about.

"Here, I made this for you," Joie said, presenting Nanci with a little box with an angel on top. "It's called an Angel Blessing Box. If someone is in trouble, if they need your help, you write their name on a piece of paper and put it in this box. Then you say a prayer to the angels to take care of them."

"Ooh boy!" Jimmy said. "Angel blessings. You two sound like a couple of kooks."

He was intrigued, Nanci could tell; otherwise why would he spend so much time listening to them?

Nanci had always had a strong faith. She had always believed in God, the higher power, but she had always resisted the hypocrisy she saw in the Catholic religion that she was raised with. She could never forget her mother throwing away the birth control pills and then urging her to have an abortion when she got pregnant. She didn't like the intolerance of other religions; she liked to think that if she wanted to, she could visit a Protestant church or a synagogue. And she started to explore other religions. She became interested in Buddhism. She became interested in goddesses. Since she had come back from Ireland, she had felt a strong pull toward her Celtic roots and all the mystical magic that came with it.

And then her sister Joie introduced her to angels, and she came to believe in their spiritual power, and the possibility of miracles. Joie took her to an all-day angel workshop at a New Age institute and Nanci listened in amazement to people telling angel stories. She had had no idea that there were so many different kinds of angels—archangels, angels that protect you, angels to whom you could pray for health and help in relationships.

But whenever she tried to involve Jimmy in what she and Joie were doing, he always said, "Believe what you want to believe, but don't involve me."

But the angels were important to Nanci. She had always felt that there was somebody

watching out for her, and she knew that an angel had to have been watching out for Jason,
otherwise he wouldn't even be there today.
Her mind began to wander, thinking about the
time before he was in rehab, how he had been
doing all those drugs, how he had been so
reckless on the motorcycle Jimmy had bought
him. She thought back to the time they had
been counseled by Connie and Ruth, who had
said, "Don't try to solve Jason's problems by
buying him presents." And that was exactly
what Jimmy had done—gone out and bought
Jason the bike he wanted. Jason's angel had to
have been on a suicide watch, Nanci thought.
Thank God those times were behind them.

One day she saw an ad in the local paper.

LOOKING FOR YOUR SPIRITUALITY?
COME TO A BOOK GROUP FRIDAY NIGHT. CALL . . .

It seemed like the ad was speaking directly
to her. She cut it out and stuck it on the fridge.
Jimmy raised his eyebrows. *Ooh boy!*

She called the number and heard the rich,
deep voice of what sounded like a very wise
old man.

* * *

There were two men who had changed her life, Nanci would realize later on. Jimmy was the first. And Charlie Raebeck would be the second.

His house, where he held his book group and his counseling practice, was on Atlantic Avenue, a wide, tree-lined road that led from the fire station all the way down to the ocean. Standing outside his house and looking down the hill, it seemed as if his road was disappearing into the sea itself.

Charlie was in his seventies. He was very tall with white hair and smiling eyes. The first thing Nanci noticed was that he had a great smile. He was friendly and demonstrative and instantly she felt at home.

He produced a book called *The Soul's Code* by James Hillman. Everyone had to read the first chapter on their own and then come back the following Friday and discuss it. From the book, Nanci learned that everyone had something called a *daemon*, an inner force that you were born with. It was the reason you were a poet or an inventor and the reason why you had been born to the parents that you were born to. It was this force inside you that made you who you were, and it was the reason why even under difficult circumstances, people would strive to satisfy whatever creative need they had.

At the start of the group there were ten people, but pretty soon this number came down to four.

Charlie's wife, Audrey, was younger than him and beautiful. Nanci was struck by her exquisite eyes—blue and almond shaped. She and Charlie kept themselves in great shape walking and running along the beach, and, Nanci noticed each time she went there, they were still deeply in love with one another.

There were ten sessions and after the ninth Jimmy suddenly asked if he could join the book group.

"There's no point joining the book club at this late stage," Nanci told him. "But if you want to go see Charlie, here's his number."

She never thought he would call. She had assumed that it was like all the other times he had listened in on her conversations with Joie. He had heard her telling Joie about Charlie, and he was curious.

So she was stunned when he said casually

the following week, "Oh, I called Charlie Rae-beck and I have an appointment to see him in a couple of days."

She thought about it for some time and worked out what it was that had driven him to seek Charlie's help. They had been arguing for the longest time, and during their most recent fight—*We're not getting anywhere, I'm not happy, you're defending yourself and putting it back on me*—they'd gone round and round till they were exhausted. Finally Jimmy had said, "Well, it's not as if we're talking about divorce."

And without missing a beat she replied, "I think that's what I *am* talking about."

So finally Jimmy had seen how serious she was. It was the first time the word "divorce" had actually come up.

And now it was her turn to stand on the sidelines and observe. She was thrilled to see how hard Jimmy worked with Charlie. This was a whole new area for him. His sessions with Charlie were private, but she watched him do his "homework" and she saw the books that he was reading. She had not actually had counseling with Charlie herself, but she knew what kinds of things Charlie talked about.

She could picture Jimmy sitting in a chair beside Charlie as she had done at the book group. Nanci knew that however cynical Jimmy might be feeling when he entered Charlie's house, when he left it, he would be totally relaxed. She also knew that Jimmy would learn about his ego, that to get along with someone in a relationship, he couldn't always be feeding his ego. He didn't always have to be right, he didn't always have to fight to the death. Instead of always attacking, he should listen. All too often she and Jimmy would talk for two hours, and at the end of it she'd realize that he hadn't listened to anything she had said because he had been too busy thinking about how to defend himself. He had to learn how to communicate, he had to learn how to agree to disagree. And, she hoped, he would learn how much his job was affecting his personality. Even though he didn't have the uniform on, when he came home, Jimmy was still very much the cop, he was giving everybody orders, and every now and then Nanci had to remind him, "You know, you're not at work."

One night she was curled up on the couch watching a video when he stood in front of the television and asked, "Can we talk?"

Ordinarily she would have been furious at the interruption. But for some time now she had been aware of a subtle change in Jimmy, and she sensed that he had something important to say.

He sat down beside her and took her hand, something he had not done for a long time.

"I want to say I'm sorry. For everything. For the way I used to complain about working all the time. I am sorry I did not realize how important the job of raising our sons was to you. I want to thank you for being there for me, for keeping everything together.

"I realize now that everybody's different. Jason and I are different and he isn't like Eric either. Not everyone has to be a jock like me. Everyone has their strengths and weaknesses. I used to think Jason was doing it on purpose when he couldn't understand his math homework, but now I understand he wasn't. I really want to apologize, Nanci. More than anything, I do not want us to divorce."

Nanci couldn't believe what she was hearing. She stretched out on the couch and laid her head in his lap. He lifted some strands of hair away from her forehead and began to braid them. It was a special thing he did in memory of their wedding day, when she had worn her hair parted in the middle with two tiny plaits caught at the back of her head in a ribbon. His touch was so soft and gentle. When he had finished, he began to stroke her forehead and caress her face all over until she was ready to melt. He turned her over so that she was looking up into his eyes.

"I don't want a divorce anymore, Jimmy."

"And you won't leave me?"

"Of course not."

"I love you, Nan." His pet name for her.

"I love you too, Jim. I want us to stay together."

He stopped going to see Charlie.

And this, Nanci would realize later, was his biggest mistake.

$\mathcal{H}$e came to see me on a mission," Charlie told her three years later as she sat beside him. "And when his mission was accomplished, he stopped coming."

"What was the mission?" Nanci asked.

"To get you back. Once he knew he had you back, little by little he stopped trying to make your marriage work. He didn't realize what he was doing, but he did it nevertheless. And now you're here."

She had called him the week before.

"I need to come and see you. Not for a book group. For me. As soon as possible."

When she walked into Charlie's comfortable welcoming house she told him, "I want to get a divorce."

"I'm sorry to hear that. What's going on?" Charlie was very calm. "Tell me how you came to this decision."

It helped that he knew their background.

"I've been going over the same things and having the same fights for too long. There's nothing there anymore," she said, bursting into tears. "I can't make him understand that the marriage has to come first, before his work, before everything. I feel like I'm screaming from the rooftops and still not getting through to him."

"You don't feel the love?" Charlie asked gently.

"No!" she said emphatically. "I feel totally isolated. He's bought these lizards and he's built them cages down in our basement. He's breeding them and he spends all his time down there. I feel like he's married to them rather than me. I know that sounds crazy but everything has gotten to be too much for me. I can't handle it anymore."

"Fine," Charlie said. "You're here and I'll help you on your path to wherever you want it to lead you. We'll talk and walk in that direction and we'll see whatever we will see."

She had expected him to say, *Are you sure this is what you want?* and to try to talk her out of it.

"I don't want papers and lawyers and the whole business of divorce. It makes me uncomfortable. I don't want anything. I don't want the house. I don't want money. I just want my freedom."

"Well," Charlie said, looking at her, "that's all well and good, but that's not usually the way it works. But it doesn't have to be ugly or bitter. People do that to themselves. What you can do is get a mediator."

Well, this is it, she thought as she walked down the path from Charlie's house. *I've taken this step, now I have to go through with it.*

And she wept all the way home.

That year, for the first time ever she did not go to his parents' Fourth of July celebration. Everyone went, all her sisters-in-law, all the kids, the cousins. They always had their own family fireworks display over the water by the house. It went on for hours and there was singing by the bonfire. Nanci usually made daquiris. But it had gotten to the stage where she was mad at his brothers and the time he spent with them.

It hurt Jimmy very deeply that she did not go.

At first he pleaded with her, "You have to come, we always go." He knew that if she didn't go, his whole family would know something was wrong between them. Nanci lied to Barbara Jean and said she had a catering job, but she knew that nobody was fooled.

Jimmy held on to his hurt forever and after a while he stopped talking about the Fourth of July. The rift between them deepened. She got a job in a shelter for abused women and began to spend a lot of time there. She worked in child care, looking after the children of the women in the shelter. She did music and played games with them during the day, and at night she worked the phones, taking hotline calls, talking to women in distress.

She welcomed the distraction of these women's problems. Anything to take her mind off the fact that however much she loved Jimmy, she was failing in her attempt to save their marriage.

Summer turned to fall. Soon it would be Thanksgiving. Nanci went into the city for her sister's wedding shower, and Jimmy called her one night while she was there.

It was like the Spanish Inquisition.

"Nanci, what are you doing there? When are you coming home? Did you dream of me last night?"

It was a strange question and she acted like she didn't hear it.

"Jimmy, why are you calling me? Can't I just be here without you calling and checking up on me all the time?"

"But did you dream about me?" he persisted. He sounded desperate.

"Jimmy, I don't know if I even dreamed at all last night."

She hung up on him. She was mad and resentful that he hated the fact that she had become independent. He might ask if she dreamed about him, but it never sounded as if he missed her. It always sounded as if he didn't trust her.

The next day he drove over from where he

worked in Brooklyn to pick her up and drive her home.

It was a very quiet ride until suddenly he brought up their phone conversation.

"What was that all about? Why were you like that on the phone? What's the problem? I can't call you?"

"I just feel like I'm being checked up on," Nanci told him. "When I'm with my sisters, I'm in the moment, that's where I am, I don't want to be checked up on. When you go away, do I call you every five minutes? I don't have that need because I'm not suspicious like you. You're always going away and I never check up on you."

It escalated pretty quickly into an argument. The louder they raised their voices, the faster Jimmy drove along the Long Island Expressway, until they got pulled over by a state trooper. Jimmy wound down the window.

"I'm sorry but we're having a fight," he explained, as if it were the most normal thing in the world. Nanci was embarrassed.

"You were going over eighty miles an hour. Maybe you should pull over and calm down, because you're going to kill yourselves."

As they sat there in the car by the side of the road, Jimmy asked her, "Are you happy?"

"No, not really. We're living a lie. There you have it . . ."

"What do you mean, 'There you have it'?"

"I don't know. Maybe we should do something about it."

"What should we do?"

"I don't know. You're not happy, I'm not happy . . ."

Jimmy was silent.

"Well," she said finally, "maybe we should just call it a day and go our separate ways. We keep going round and round. We're not getting anywhere. Why should we be miserable?"

When they came off the LIE, they drove in silence along the back roads, and when they were almost home, Jimmy said quietly, "So, what are you saying? You're just going to throw away twenty-two years of marriage?"

"You know what?" Nanci said. "That's a long time and some people don't even have that. Maybe we should just feel grateful for the time we had."

And even though she had just made a decision that would rip their whole lives apart, it was like a cloud had been lifted and suddenly she saw the light. Yes, that was exactly what they would do.

They pulled into the driveway and went into the house. Once inside, they went their separate ways. Jimmy went straight to his computer. Nanci, still forever studying at night school whenever she could, had a paper to write on Elizabeth I for her history class. As she wrote furiously into the night, all of her pent-up energy went into writing about the independent daughter of Henry VIII. She finished in the middle of the night and went to bed.

But instead of getting into the bed she had shared with Jimmy for so many years, she automatically slipped into the guest room. She didn't think twice about it: it was as if a wall had come down between them.

In the coming weeks she spoke of renting an apartment in Sag Harbor, but, as Jimmy pointed out, neither of them could afford to move out.

So she stayed in the guest room, and as they entered the month of December, she lay awake every night wondering, *How will we ever get through Christmas?*

FOURTEEN

❦

Christmas Day was like a funeral. At a funeral, people were gathered together because someone had died, and it was supposed to be a sad occasion, but even so everyone always ate and drank a lot. So it was with them on Christmas Day. Their marriage was dead, Nanci observed, but there still had to be some sort of forced celebration. Everything felt so strained and awkward. She only hoped the boys weren't too upset underneath everything. She had tried to explain what was happening to Eric one morning while driving him to school, but he had brushed her aside.

"Look, Mom, it's your business." Like all the

LaGarenne men, he didn't have an easy time with emotion.

She worried about him. He had always been so sensitive; he had to have picked up on what was going on. And then Jason had called one night out of the blue to ask what was happening. He was away at college by now, a changed person.

"Listen," he said, "I understand you have problems and I can't stop thinking about it while I'm away at school. Look, you guys need to do what you have to do and that's fine, that's your business. But understand that it's not just about you, it's affecting the whole family, and I'm worried about Eric. And in case you've forgotten, I'm supposed to be going away to Australia for six months right after Christmas. Should I cancel my trip? Something tells me maybe I ought to stay home."

Through her misery, Nanci marveled at how sensitive and caring Jason had become. She felt guilty that her problems were affecting the boys.

They had talked him out of it. It was his big chance. He had to go to Australia. And when he came home for Christmas, Nanci was touched to see how much time he spent with

Eric, taking him out on brotherly bonding sessions. Eric didn't talk much, wasn't one to give much away about how he was feeling no matter how sensitive he was, but at least she knew he had Jason watching out for him.

"Hey, Mom?" They were calling her now. "Can we take the van? We want to go over to Grandma's house to give her and Grandpa our presents. You'll come later, right?"

She barely answered, barely heard them leave the house.

Here she was on Christmas night, sitting by the fireplace she loved so much, surrounded by her burning candles, the old quilt Jimmy had brought her back from Texas, her books, the scent wafting from a lighted incense stick. It was then that Jimmy had walked in with his bottle of wine and the divorce papers. It was the loneliest moment of their lives together. In all their twenty-two years of marriage, even in the ugliest moments, Nanci had never once really believed she would be reading divorce papers.

"Why are you looking at them like that?" Jimmy was agitated, on his feet again, walking in and out of the kitchen.

She looked at the paperwork. She had never

seen a legal document before, except when they had bought their house, and then Jimmy had dealt with it. *So many pages*, was her first thought. And then, as she began to read, the legal jargon hit her like a sledgehammer.

The first party, the second party, the children, the minor child, the son of who will reside with, the property of, the dissolution of the marriage . . .

This was all legal mumbo jumbo, this had nothing to do with them.

"I don't understand why we need these papers," she said.

"What is it you don't understand?" Jimmy was standing by the kitchen counter.

"I don't understand why these papers are here."

He came and sat down next to her. "What do you mean? Isn't this what you wanted? I thought this was what you wanted?"

It was true. She'd essentially told him she was ready for a divorce. Still, it was a shock to see it in writing.

All the words were blurred, swimming before her eyes in a pool of water, and she realized that her tears were falling on the papers. She pushed the papers away from her.

"We have to sign papers," Jimmy told her. "We can't just say I'll go my way and you'll go your way and everything will be great. It doesn't work like that."

"I don't mean that," Nanci cried. "I don't want this divorce."

"What did you say?"

"I don't want this divorce. I still love you."

Jimmy looked at her as if she was speaking another language. And then the floodgates opened and she began to sob. Loud, heartrending sobs and she could not stop.

When she heard Jimmy begin to cry, she reached out her arms to him.

"What happened to us?" she whispered. "We came so close."

"We just forgot what we meant to each other. Now we have to try and remember. I love you, Nanci. I never wanted a divorce. You were the one who—"

"I know, I know. But I didn't want *this* . . ."

She pointed to the papers lying on the table. Jimmy got up to get them some tissues to dry their eyes, and when he returned, he picked up the papers.

"You've just told me what you think of

these," he said, waving them in the air. "Well, this is what I think of them." And he threw them into the flames in the fireplace.

He opened another bottle of wine and dimmed the lights.

"When I looked at you just now as I handed you the papers, for a second I saw you as you were on our wedding day. I saw you standing there waiting for me at the top of the aisle with your hair plaited behind your head and your beautiful cream dress with the transparent sleeves. And you looked so young and precious to me, I knew I had to come up that aisle and take care of you forever.

"That's why I got up and went to stand in the kitchen just now, this situation was just too painful. I knew if I sat there a minute longer, I would start to cry. I believed you wanted these divorce papers, and if that was what you wanted, I thought I had to go through with it."

He seemed about to place an arm around her shoulder, but he stopped and looked at her, as if he wasn't quite sure.

Nanci gave him her answer by snuggling into his embrace.

"It was like our whole life was just this piece of paper, and I just couldn't bear it," she said.

"Our whole life is everything we experience to-gether, not a contract broken down to itemize who gets money and who gets property."

"I know what you mean. When I read them, I thought, 'If Nanci gets the kids and the house and I get the pigs and the animals, who gets our friends?' Think of our friend Gail, she's pre-cious to both of us. I thought, 'Who gets Gail?' "

"I met her first," Nanci said.

"Oh, you did, did you? Well, we can play this game all night: Who gets the mailman? Who gets that squirrel who hops across the deck every morning?"

"Seriously, Jimmy, I've hated the atmosphere in this house."

"Me too. When I woke up this morning, I thought it was going to be the worst Christmas I'd ever have, but look what's happened. It's turned out to be one of the best because we didn't sign the papers. This morning we were going to get divorced and now we're not. It's the best Christmas present you could have given me."

He leaned over and kissed her neck in a place he knew she was always ticklish, and soon he had succeeded in forcing her tears to make way for laughter.

"That's better," he said, "now I can kiss you properly."

They sat up way into the night, talking round and round, going over all the problems of the last few months. But this time, instead of getting nowhere, they moved forward to embrace each other in newfound love.

Later, when they had finally gone upstairs to consummate their reunion, together again in their bedroom, Jimmy said, "I've missed you so much. I've thought of you lying there in the spare room. And see, even after all this time, that's the beauty of our relationship, it feels so intense and beautiful that we never just have sex, whenever we're together we always make love. Even when we were still arguing by day and still sharing a bed at night, we always made love, not sex. That's what made me believe that it would always work out one day."

Nanci burrowed her face in his neck and whispered what she always said to him after they made love.

"I love you, James."

And now the hard work would really begin.

Nanci had an appointment with Charlie between Christmas and New Year, and the minute she walked in, he knew something had happened. She often wondered if he was clairvoyant.

"So, you look well rested and you have a big smile on your face. Did you have a good Christmas?"

"Charlie, I've decided I don't want to get a divorce after all."

"Oh," he said, giving her one of his warm smiles, "we've opened your heart."

She had not realized how angry she was when she first went to see Charlie. She wasn't outwardly angry but she was being eaten up on the inside.

She had spent long periods at home by the fire reading and letting Charlie's wisdom fill her thoughts. It wasn't her nature to be so unloving. Charlie allowed her to rediscover herself, to let go of her ego and open her heart. She had not realized her heart was closed; she had thought she was angry with Jimmy, that she didn't want Jimmy in her life. It wasn't that her heart was completely closed, it was just that a part of it was closed to him and she had not understood how that was affecting her whole self.

"You were so intense when you first came

here," Charlie told her. "You said that divorce was what you wanted. You needed my help to proceed with that. I had to accompany you on the journey you were making, even though I wasn't sure that was where it should or would lead. Now you're on this journey to discover yourself, and you'll continue that because your heart is open and you're a loving person. You're who you really are. When your heart is closed, you're going against who you are and you don't show love. Your love is conditional. When you've decided that your love is unconditional, you can be the person you are meant to be."

Charlie asked about Jimmy.

"He's thrilled of course. He genuinely is. But to be honest with you, Charlie, this morning he wondered out loud if it would last. I know I will never change my mind again, but although he was overjoyed on Christmas Day, I sensed this morning that he was a little bit afraid of my change of heart, as if he didn't quite believe it."

"Well, that's natural," Charlie said. "Don't forget he came to see me on a mission to get you back when you first talked about divorce. And then you closed your heart to him again."

"Well, that's because he went back to working long hours and . . ."

She saw Charlie looking at her. "Oh, I see what you're saying. It has nothing to do with Jimmy."

Through Charlie she had learned the independence and empowering of herself as a woman that she had been striving for ever since she was a teenager. She had learned that she didn't have to be this angry person who was afraid to show her softer side. She had learned to surrender, to be at one with her spirit and who she was inside. She learned to surrender the false armor in which she had been trapped. She had thought she could not be this woman with Jimmy holding her back, but then she had learned it was not like that. It had nothing to do with Jimmy. She was holding herself back. Being independent and her own person and being angry with Jimmy were two totally different things, and the same went for loving him.

She wished she had remembered all this when she had said goodbye to Jimmy that morning. He was going away for New Year's. It was a trip that had been planned for some time; he was going scuba diving with his brother Harold. It would be the first New Year's they had ever spent apart since they had been together. Of course, it had been planned way before Christmas, when they were barely speaking to each other. Now Jimmy was wondering whether he should still go.

"Of course you should go," Nanci said. "You can't disappoint your brother. He's been looking forward to it. So have you. Go! I'll be fine."

"I'll call you New Year's Eve and we'll talk and we'll see the New Year in over the phone."

But as she kissed him goodbye she sensed that he was still reluctant to go, and she wondered if she should have insisted he stay with her. Maybe that was what he was looking for? Some kind of reassurance that she wanted him with her.

Over the next couple of days, she worked some extra hours at the shelter. It was her time with these children of abused women that had kept her sane over the last few months. As she listened to the women's stories, they made her own problems seem tiny by comparison.

Jimmy called the night before New Year's.

"How are you? Where are you?" she asked.

"I'm here," he said.

"Where's here?"

"Here's here," he said, laughing. "We're not diving because it's too cold."

"Well, call me tomorrow on New Year's Eve."

"Sure."

"And Jimmy, I love—"

But he was gone.

On New Year's Eve she rented some videos and planned an early night because she had an early start at the shelter the next day.

She got into bed with the phone beside her, expecting Jimmy's call at any minute.

On an impulse she decided to start a new journal that would be a celebration of their reunion. Her sister Joie had given her a beautifully bound book for Christmas, and Nanci felt this would make the perfect journal.

She opened the first page and began to write.

James,
I miss you. I love you. You are the other side of my soul in the darkness. I was afraid the light was gone forever.

I forgot the light was inside me waiting to shine my love and dreams and friendship on you.

I just wanted to be your best friend the whole time.

Maybe you can help me live more freely and I can help you love your spirit. We both have our strengths.

I have found my heart again. It was there all along. It just needed a good dusting. Now it is wide open.

I love you. I forgive you. I forgive myself. Can you do the same?

Nan

The phone rang and she nearly fell out of bed in her rush to answer it.

"Jimmy?"

But it was Joie calling from Staten Island to wish her a happy New Year. She was all bubbly. Nanci wondered if she was calling from a party.

"Has Jimmy called yet?"

"No, not yet," Nanci said.

"Oh, he will."

"Joie, guess what? I used the beautiful book you gave me to start a new journal. I've just written my first entry—a letter to Jimmy."

"Well, leave it out for him to see when he gets home and maybe he'll reply," Joie suggested.

"That's such a great idea." Nanci hung up and laid her letter to Jimmy open on his pillow. When he called, she would rest her head beside it, and it would be as if he were there with her.

She cried a little. She missed him. It had been a mistake to send him away. She didn't even know where he was, so she couldn't call him to tell him she missed him.

She fell asleep a little before midnight, thinking, *The phone will wake me when he calls.*

*B*ut history has a habit of repeating itself.

What is it with us and New Year's Eve? Nanci wondered when she woke up the next morning and realized Jimmy had not called her. She could still remember that fateful New Year's Eve twenty-six years ago when Jimmy had asked her to go steady and then been unavailable when she had tried to give him her answer.

Nanci sat up in bed and hugged herself. Should she be worried that he hadn't called? No, she decided, she shouldn't. She knew he loved her. And she also knew that sometimes he wasn't too great on details. In a way, it was fitting that the same thing had happened all those years ago. It was almost as if they had been transported back to that time when they were only sixteen and given a chance to start afresh.

And just like then, it began with Jimmy asking her out on a date. . . .

FIFTEEN

❦

For the longest time, Nanci had used an old electric typewriter, but when it finally gave up the ghost, she was forced to turn to the computer. She had resisted the Internet because the only way she saw it being used was when Jimmy spent hours and hours upstairs playing computer games. It evoked a sad time for her, one she did not care to dwell upon, so to begin with she only used the word-processing program on the computer to do her writing.

But, as Jimmy pointed out, soon they would be entering a new century. He insisted she learn to use e-mail. He helped her set up with her password and went off to work, telling her to look for an e-mail from him later in the day.

The first e-mail Nanci received was from her husband—asking her for a date.

Hi Nanci!
I'd love to take you out to dinner on Friday.
Would you be available to go out on a date
with me? Maybe we could go to this restau-
rant I know in Montauk. And then we could
go to a friendly bar. How about it?

Jimmy

Nanci smiled. She had forgiven him for not calling on New Year's Eve.

Now he was home and he wanted a date.

She ordered some lingerie and a short black dress from Victoria's Secret. She put on a little blue cardigan to protect her from the bitter January cold, and her tall black boots. She felt good about herself. The only beneficial thing about the stress she had suffered over the past few months was that she had lost a lot of weight.

Standing there on Friday night, waiting to go out with her husband, Nanci had serious butterflies in her stomach. Since they had thrown the divorce papers into the fire, she had looked at him differently. It was simple. She was falling in love with him again.

They had dinner at the Surfside Inn, from which they could see the winter ocean pounding onto the beach.

"You've got a twinkle in your eye tonight," Jimmy told her. "Now I'm going to take you to a bar."

He took her to the Memory, a bar that had been immortalized in a song by the Rolling Stones. Legend had it that Mick Jagger had stayed at the Memory and written the song because he liked it so much.

Nanci was thrilled. "I haven't been here in years. Remember when we were teenagers and we used to come here to shoot pool? It looks exactly the same."

"I brought you here for a special reason," Jimmy told her, leading her to a table. "Do you remember that time we went on vacation in North Carolina with my brother and his wife and we all sang karaoke?"

Nanci nodded. They had all been very drunk, she recalled.

"Well, I went to a karaoke bar in Texas and I've been practicing," Jimmy said. "I wanted to surprise you. They have karaoke here."

And then, to her amazement, he walked over to the man who was doing the karaoke and gave him a request. Then he took the microphone and began to sing.

To begin with, he sang to everyone in the bar. Nanci had always known he had a great voice, rich, deep, reaching out to the far corners of the room. He sang a Willie Nelson song, "Always on My Mind."

And then he turned toward her and began to sing the song directly to her, and there was no mistaking the message he was trying to convey. Everyone in the bar was watching them and saying "Aaaah! That's so cute!"

"Come and sing with me," he mouthed at her.

But Nanci was too shy. She went to him and he held her in his arms while they danced together far into the night.

So their first date was dinner and dancing. Nanci wondered what the second date would be.

He took her to the movies. They saw a film called *Playing by Heart* about three sisters and their very strong father. The sisters came home for their father's birthday and, while they were there, sorted out all their issues.

Nanci found it very moving and she was close to tears when they walked out of the movie theater.

Jimmy took her for a drink and as they talked, Nanci sensed how tentative they were around each other. It didn't worry her. She found it interesting that they were behaving exactly as if they were dating, as if they wanted to get to know each other better but did not quite know how the other felt.

It was fun. It was intriguing. It was if they were rediscovering each other.

If she only knew!

"So, how are you?" Jimmy asked her.

"I'm doing great. I love my work at the shelter, the way I can help those poor abused women. It makes me realize how lucky I've been with my life. Whatever problems I may have had, they were nothing compared to what these women have had to put up with."

"I'm glad to hear it." Jimmy looked at her warily. "It's good to spend time with you, Nanci. We've been apart for so long. When I was at the house, you were always gone, at your sister's or at Molly's. And I guess when I was working weekends, you were there."

"Yes. I planned it deliberately. I didn't want to be there with you. I was so angry with you." Nanci felt she was talking about a stranger, though she didn't feel angry with Jimmy anymore. "When we were separated and I wasn't home—and you weren't either—I often wondered where you stayed. I know sometimes it was at work, but where else did you go?"

"Oh, you know, I stayed with friends."

"You did? Which friends? I never called because I didn't want to feel like I was checking up on you."

"Oh, a whole bunch of friends."

"A whole bunch? Our friends?"

He shook his head.

"So, these friends—men or women?"

"A woman."

A *woman*. Singular. Nanci's heart skipped a beat.

"A woman?"

"Yes."

"Well, does she live around here?"

"No."

"Where did you meet her?"

"Texas."

Nanci took a deep breath. She couldn't ask.

But she had to.

"Did you sleep with her?"

"Yes."

Yes! He had said yes. She couldn't look at him. She had asked the question but she had not been prepared for the answer. She waited for him to reassure her that this woman meant nothing to him, and when he didn't say anything, she sneaked a look at him. He was staring at her, his face terrifyingly solemn. So she wrestled with the urge to cry out at him and forced herself to stay calm and ask a practical question instead.

"Did you use a condom?"

"Yes."

"What's her name?"

"Jennifer."

"Can I have another glass of wine, please?"

Nanci had never had a good head for liquor. And she hadn't had anything to eat. The last thing she should be doing was drinking another glass of wine.

Jimmy was watching her closely. It was like that time before they were married when she had found him with Lola at the Panoramic right here on Montauk. On the surface it probably looked as if she was taking it all in her stride. She gave no outward sign of how much she was reeling inside.

"You know," she said, sipping her wine, "I can understand you doing that, because when I was in Ireland, I met somebody."

"You *did*?" Unlike her, Jimmy's face showed how much she'd shaken him with her revelation.

"Yes. I didn't sleep with this guy—but I kissed him."

"You know, I've always wondered what happened over there. Before you went, I was convinced you were going to meet someone and never come back. You had this whole Celtic thing going on, and I wasn't part of it. It made me feel so insecure."

Through the pain she was feeling about his revelation, another line of thought began to occur to her. It really hadn't dawned on her that she'd been abandoning him, or that he would have cared. She'd been so focused on how she herself had been wronged.

"So you know how it feels when you're not appreciated," she said, looking him in the eye, "then you meet someone new and start getting the attention that you're maybe not getting at home. Suddenly somebody thinks you're the greatest thing since sliced bread. They don't live with you, so they don't know all your annoying habits. And they look at you as if you're the most beautiful thing they've ever seen. It was nice to have the attention." She paused. Had it been like that for him? Was that why he had betrayed her with someone else? She desperately needed some kind of reassurance from him. "So I guess I can see what happened when you met your *friend*. What was she like?"

Nanci couldn't believe that she was sitting here with her husband, talking about another woman, as if they were just friends discussing their lives—which in a way they were.

"She was tall, about your height. Her hair was a little lighter. She had those—what do you call them? Highlights." *Blonde*, thought Nanci, *the total opposite of me*. Jimmy seemed relieved to be talking about this, she noticed. He'd obviously been weighted down by guilt about her for a long time. When he'd seen that Nanci didn't slam down her wineglass and storm out of the bar, it was as if the floodgates had been opened. He couldn't stop talking about her, until finally he went one step too far.

"She's really nice," he said. "You'd like her, Nanci. I'm sure if the two of you met up, you'd be friends."

Suddenly Nanci had had enough.

"New Year's," she said, "when you didn't call. Were you with her?"

He nodded.

"Are you still talking to her?"

She was shaking as she waited for his answer.

"Yes, I am."

Now she did get up and leave the bar, and Jimmy ran after her.

When they got home, she went straight to the bathroom and threw up. She didn't know if it was because of the wine or a reaction to the conversation, as if she just wanted to get all the information she'd received out of her system.

Jimmy came into the bathroom behind her and stood over her, holding her long dark hair out of her face and stroking her forehead while she vomited.

"Leave me," she told him, "leave me. I'm fine."

But he picked her up and gently carried her to bed.

When she woke up the next morning, he had already left for work, but there, on the pillow beside her, was the journal.

She picked it up and saw that he had replied to what she had written on New Year's Eve.

Nan,
I hear your thoughts and I feel your love. Can we make the future different from the past? I'm afraid of making the same mistakes again.

It's not you. It's the job, the bills, the crap I deal with. I want us to go to the next height of love, the forever . . .

I have to work through this. I don't want to just love you, I want to see you as my sun, to need you again. . . .

James

She read it through several times. On the one hand, she wondered what he meant by "I have to work through this." Did he mean he had to work through the thing with Jennifer, whoever she was? On the other hand, what he wrote was sweetness itself. Last night she had been ready to go back to the spare room. But now in the cold light of morning, reading his words of love, she knew she wanted to forgive him.

They had to move forward. In the journal, he had not mentioned Jennifer or the man she had met in Ireland. And she felt this was deliberate. They would put this episode behind them.

She picked up a pen and began to write.

James,
I read your words and I understand. I've felt the same feelings with the everyday stuff draining me. I felt your absence from my life, and mine from yours.

We both need to value, respect, and communicate with each other more. I'm sorry for my part.

I have always believed in hope and that has gotten me through difficult times in my life— and in ours too.

I will continue to have hope and love. That is living. Everything else is a gift.

Hope and love, baby
Nan

As an afterthought, she decided to give the journal a title. Turning it over, she thought for a moment, then wrote on the cover the words "A

Marriage Restored." Then she placed it once again on Jimmy's pillow.

She felt as if he had made a proposal and she wanted him to see her answer.

SIXTEEN

❦

I'm afraid of making the same mistakes twice.

Nanci was full of hope that they were on the right track, but that line, more than any other in Jimmy's journal entry, still haunted Nanci over the next few days.

She was absolutely sure that to be with Jimmy and love him forever was what she wanted more than anything else in the world. She forgave him his time with Jennifer. She understood what that had been about. She knew Jimmy loved her. She could see new evidence of this every day. But what she could also see was that he was very scared.

* * *

Old Hither Hills was their new dating spot. They had an old four-by-four pickup truck and it had become an evening ritual when the weather was clear to go and watch the sun set. There was nothing like a winter sunset when the sun was a brilliant crimson ball outlined against a gray-blue sky, sinking over snow-capped dunes and icy water. The only way to get to Old Hither Hills was to take a truck and drive down an old dirt road over the railroad tracks. It led up to the crest of a bluff where you could park and look out over Gardiner's Bay.

It was very private, especially in winter. They took a picnic and parked. Jimmy often brought along his guitar, and he sat strumming and singing to her while she rested her head on his shoulder. Sometimes they just huddled close to ward off the cold outside, and looked out over the bay, enjoying the comfort of silence.

And sometimes they talked.

"This is so great," Jimmy would say.

"It's perfect," she'd whisper back.

But then he'd always add something like "But how do we know it'll stay like this? How do we know we'll still be like this in six months?"

"We don't know," Nanci said, "but then we've never known. Our life is what we make it. I know this is who I am and who I am meant to be. We have a future together but it's going to be different—because we're different now. We're dating again, we're reaching out and showing each other our love. We're paying attention to the relationship. We've finally decided that our relationship is the most important thing. But it's not like there's an instant cure. You have to keep working at it."

"I know, I know," he said. Nanci hugged him closer to her. Sometimes he sounded so anguished. "Every day, when I'm driving to work for two hours along the Long Island Expressway, I have time to think and go over what's happened between us. In the past I would be seething with resentment that I had to be trapped in a car for so long while you could be enjoying the freedom of our house and the beach. Recently, I've been working on convincing myself that all that is in the past."

Nanci nodded. More and more, she had come to realize that he'd been suffering just as much as she had.

Jimmy went on, "But then I arrive at work and there are guys in the unit telling me you're a bitch, that you only want to be with me for my pension. They're telling me I've worked my ass off for all these years and I deserve to do whatever I want. I can have it all. They're saying you'll take me back and then you'll take everything we have."

"So what did you say to them?" Nanci held her breath. She could hear the subtext. *Ditch the wife, stick with the girlfriend.* She knew a lot of the men he worked with. Some of them were real stand-up guys who'd been out to the house, even dated her sister, but the others were trouble. Divorced, disillusioned, they wanted to reclaim Jimmy as one of their own, for all the wrong reasons.

"I told them it wasn't like that," he said. "I told them we were sleeping in separate rooms for a while but it was an amicable separation. I told them we were friendly, and it's true, we were. But we were too friendly. In a way, we were tiptoeing around each other all the time. I was afraid to say anything in case it led to a fight."

"Me too," Nanci agreed, "but now it's okay. We don't have to be afraid to say anything anymore. We can talk."

Jimmy's eyes were on the point of tears. The way he was able to show her his emotion had been what had made her fall in love with him, Nanci remembered—and it was one of many reasons why she was still in love with him.

"It's like you were on the other side of the field and I'd be wondering, 'Where's my teammate?'"

"Your teammate was right there all along," Nanci told him softly, moved by his words. "You just had to look for her. And now, you just have to believe she'll always be there with you. Don't listen to the guys at work. Close your ears to all negative thoughts. Listen to your heart. Believe in yourself and believe in hope."

They moved on from their sunset dating at Old Hither Hills to breakfast dating. They started the day by making wonderful early-morning love. Nanci woke to the soft touch of Jimmy's fingers tracing the outline of her face in the dawn light. Then he kissed her neck where he knew she was ticklish, and she rolled over, laughing, into his arms.

At the end of their lovemaking, they had their tender ritual. Jimmy always said with total wonder, as if he had only just discovered it, "See, isn't it amazing, we never just have sex . . . we always make love."

Nanci always replied, "I love you, James."

Afterwards they'd go to a café for breakfast. They'd drive two cars so that after breakfast, Jimmy could kiss her goodbye and go straight to work in Brooklyn.

"It's crazy how getting worn down by life can drive two people apart," he told her one morning. "I heard on the car radio yesterday that 60 percent of the population of America is divorced."

"Not us," Nanci said.

"No way," Jimmy said, laughing. "I'm in the rescue business. I rescue people in my helicopter and I'm going to rescue my marriage."

Nanci smiled. *Her hero to the rescue!*

"I'm like Wrong Way Corrigan, remember I told you about him? Well, like him I just took a wrong turn. Now I'm back on track. See you tonight."

It was a magical time, but it was bittersweet. Try as he might, Jimmy still could not shake off his doubts. It seemed as soon as he left her and arrived at work, he was uncertain once again. He e-mailed her constantly throughout the day. The same old questions. *How can I be sure? How do we know this will last?* The words were so different from his journal entries. Their anniversary was coming up in February, and Nanci felt the need to resolve the situation before then.

One day she found herself at Charlie's house, needing some advice from the counselor she trusted most.

"He's badly hurt," Charlie explained. "Don't forget that when he came to see me, it was on this mission to get you back."

"And then when he got me back, he retreated once again," Nanci said.

"Exactly. He knows what he did. Now he wonders if you will do the same. He's frightened that your new loving feeling won't last, that you'll retreat from him. The way you did before. You have to show him it will. That's all you can do."

"I know," Nanci said quietly.

She knew of one way to show him what he meant to her. They had talked about what they would do when Jimmy retired from the police force. He didn't want to do security anymore because it meant they'd be separated so much. They had to search for something they could do together. He had always wondered if there was a way they could make a living with his animals. It was only the fact that all the lizards and other reptiles gave Nanci the creeps that was holding them back.

Nanci went home that day filled with determination. She had a plan. Steeling herself, she went down to the basement. She opened one of the cages and, biting her lip, forced herself to touch them. She could not quite bring herself to pick one up. She would wait for Jimmy to be with her before she did that.

When he came home that night, she was down in the basement again. She called out to him.

"Jimmy, I'm down here. In the basement with your animals."

"Doing the laundry? Will you be long?"

"No, I'm not doing laundry. Come down and see."

He came down the steps slowly.

His face when he saw her there was worth the repulsion she had felt at touching the scaly creatures. She had taken an interest in something that meant a lot to him—even though he knew it was hard for her.

She could see it meant the world to him.

And his journal entry the next morning said it all.

Nan,
Holding you this morning in such a loving way seemed perfect. We can still go through the difficult times with love. I need to know why we hurt each other. Why, when we loved each other, did it happen? I remember when I asked you out 26 years ago. That is a lifetime. Now here we are. Most people have never had what we've had. I want to be with you, not because of the past good times—no, great times—I want to be with you because I love you. I want to share my dreams and life with you. I want you to share your dreams with me.

When you got involved and touched the lizards yesterday, I said, "Well, there is hope."

There it is again. Hope.

Please hang on to it and I will too.

I want to resolve the painful times and have

our relationship be guided by love and friend-
ship. Then the communication and excitement
will come easy.

I love you,
James

And somehow after that, Nanci was no longer repulsed by the lizards. She even helped birth the chameleons and was touched by the experience. They began to plan the lizard shows they would do together. They would take the animals to schools, Cub Scouts, birthday parties. They would show the kids the lizards, let them pet them like they did, in order to learn about the endangered species and to learn how to care for them as pets, the responsibilities, the feeding, the husbandry.

"You'll walk around looking beautiful and encouraging the little children to come and learn about the lizards, just like you encourage the kids at the shelter," Jimmy said.

"And you'll do all the talking as usual," Nanci said, laughing.

Their most constant date was on Friday nights. Ever since the first time they'd gone, every Friday night they went to karaoke. Now

Nanci was singing as much as Jimmy and it was like an extension of the journal. He sang a song to her and she replied with a song to him. Pretty soon they each built up their own personal repertoire that they performed every Friday night, much to the delight of the bar crowd.

Jimmy sang Rod Stewart's "Have I Told You Lately That I Love You?" Marc Anthony's "You Sang to Me," and two John Denver songs, "Back Home Again," and "You Fill Up My Senses."

Nanci sang Carly Simon's "Nobody Does It Better," Cass Elliot's "Dream a Little Dream of Me," and two songs by the Eagles, "Love Will Keep Us Alive" and "Desperado."

Nanci played her Sarah McLachlan CD *Surfacing* while she wrote her journal entries to Jimmy. It seemed a fitting title for how she was feeling. Every day they were becoming closer, and above all, as she always told him, she had hope.

James,
Yes, the hope has kept us afloat once more. . . .
Sometimes we got tired and said, "What's the point?" I know I did. I love you and I'm

headed forward, not backward where blame, insecurity, and fear lived. I don't mean to oversimplify our situation, but for me when I saw the light, it was simple and clean.

Forgiveness is the way for me, and for us. It has made me free in a way. There is no heavy weighted-down feeling of anger, and I don't need to know the outcome immediately. I know what is important. Love. An open heart. Being available in our relationship. Our belief in each other's dreams. We forgot that for a while.

I almost lost the one person who breathes in and out of my heart: you, James.

Let's keep talking. The answers will come.

Thank God and the angels that when they spoke to my heart, I was listening.

All of me,
Nan

Finally, she felt, they were turning around. Jimmy was responding. Even his e-mails had become less uncertain.

Then the second bombshell dropped.

For her part, while she had conquered her initial fear of the computer, Nanci rarely sent e-mails. She read Jimmy's and she worked on her writing, but other than that she steered clear of the computer.

Jason, however, wanted to use the computer when he was home visiting from college.

"Dad, what's your password? I need it, I want to go on the computer."

"I never give out my password," said Jimmy. Nanci looked up, surprised. It wasn't like Jimmy to keep something from them.

"C'mon, Dad," Jason said, laughing. "What are you, a drug dealer? How come you won't give out your password?"

"That's why you have a password," Jimmy said, "It's something only you know."

He continued to withhold it and when Jason gave up and left the room in frustration, Nanci turned to Jimmy. "Why won't you tell him? Tell me. You know mine, it's only fair that I know yours."

He saw her face, knew it had become more than something between him and Jason.

He gave her his password.

Nanci wrote it down but she forgot she even had it until a few weeks later when she found it among some papers.

She knew Jimmy received a lot of e-mails. Because she so rarely used the computer, no one ever sent her mail except Jimmy. All their friends communicated with him and he relayed their messages.

She went to his mailbox, just for fun, to see who had contacted them. Maybe there'd be an invitation to a party, something to liven up the cold winter months.

She enjoyed seeing how creative their friends could be with their e-mail addresses. As she opened the mail, one by one, she laughed out loud.

And then as she clicked open a message that had come in only an hour earlier, her fingers froze over the keyboard.

Jimmy,
I miss you so much. I just want to be with you. I'd rather have pieces of you than none of you at all. Please call me. I want to come and see you. I'm thinking of making a trip to New York . . .

Nanci couldn't read any more. The words blurred before her eyes as the tears started to form.

She printed it out immediately. When he saw it, he would erase it or say it hadn't been what she thought. If she had it in her hand, she could confront him with it.

She closed the computer down and went downstairs to wait for him to come home.

*W*hen he walked in the door, she stood up and told him right away.

"Someone sent you an e-mail. A woman."

"What woman?" he said. Then he changed the subject. "What's for dinner?"

"You know what woman. She's coming to New York." Nanci was yelling now.

"What are you talking about? If you mean who I think you mean, it's over. Nobody's coming to New York."

"Oh really? Then why is she sending you an e-mail?" she screamed, totally losing her composure. For some reason, she couldn't stay calm the way she had when she had first learned about Jennifer. Perhaps it was because it was that now, unlike then, she was vulnerable. Before, her heart had been cold and closed. But in the past few months, it had become warm and open.

And vulnerable.

"You're going to have to deal with this, Jimmy, but don't feed me bullshit, because I won't stand for it. I love you. You tell me that it's over. I forgave you. But then she sends you this e-mail. Here it is. Read it and tell me what it's all about."

Jimmy read the e-mail and then he tore it up. "Nanci, I promise you I have told her it's over."

"Well, she's not getting the message. You can be pretty vague sometimes, Jimmy, because you don't like to be the bad guy. You don't want to hurt her, so maybe you've avoided telling her straight. Maybe you're just hoping she'll understand and go away and you won't have to have any kind of confrontation with her." Jimmy was shaking his head but Nanci kept going. "You can't be evasive, you have to tell her straight out. And maybe she won't like you very much for a while, but you're going to have to learn to live with that."

"I don't know what to do," Jimmy said. "It's not like that. I *did* end it. But then I wasn't sure. I knew if you did the same thing to me, if you had an affair with someone, I knew I would never be able to forgive you. So I just haven't been able to convince myself that you've forgiven me. And she kept calling me, which made it worse. I couldn't turn around to her and say 'To hell with you.'"

"Jimmy, you can't have it both ways," Nanci told him.

"I know." He looked at her. "I know that, Nan."

"I mean it, Jimmy. You can't be here with me and also have a girlfriend. I know you have doubts, I understand. But if you want it to work out between us, you have to make a total commitment to the marriage."

"That's it?"

"That's it."

After a sleepless night, she spent the next day fretting. She was tempted to go to the computer and see if there was another e-mail, but she resisted. What good would it do? She had given Jimmy an ultimatum; now there was nothing more she could do. She had begun a journey down a certain path, and she had to see where it would take her.

When Jimmy came home his first words surprised her.

"Would you be willing to lend me the little cross you wear around your neck?" he asked.

"I will. Of course I will, if you really want

it." Her fingers went to the gold chain at her throat, searching for the clasp. It was the Faith symbol on the bracelet he had given her many years ago. Significantly, she had lost the heart for Charity, but, equally significantly she felt, they still had the anchor symbolizing Hope upstairs by their bed. "But why do you want it?"

"I'm going to a retreat."

"You're *what*?" Nanci couldn't believe what she was hearing.

"I've been talking to someone at work. There's this counselor at work that the guys in trouble talk to, the alcoholics, the guys getting a divorce, the lost souls. He thinks it's what I need."

"I do too," Nanci said.

"It's a Catholic retreat and we're supposed to take a cross. I don't have one. Can I take yours?"

"Of course," Nanci said, unfastening it and placing it in the palm of his hand. This way he would have a part of her with him.

"I'll be gone for a week," Jimmy told her. "When I get back, I'll tell you whether I can commit myself to our marriage completely for good. I have to banish all the doubts once and for all, the doubts I have about myself, about whether I can trust you to forgive me, whether I can forgive myself."

He left the next day, and when he had gone, Nanci took the journal and prepared to write her reply to him. But for the first time since they had begun "A Marriage Restored," she could not write a word no matter how hard she tried.

SEVENTEEN

With her mind in turmoil, Nanci slowly closed the journal. She would open it again later when she had calmed down. She must not write when she was upset; she must wait until she felt at peace with herself.

She prepared for her morning ritual, lighting the incense and the tall white candles. She burned some sage and opened her Angel Blessing Box. Inside she found her affirmation, the words she had written to herself to read every morning: *I congratulate myself on the person I am and the person I am becoming.*

She said the words to herself a few times and then wrote Jimmy's name on a piece of paper. "Restore our marriage." She began to write, then stopped. Their marriage had already been restored. They were no longer sleeping in separate rooms; they were reaffirming their love for each other every day.

Instead she wrote, "Help Jimmy to banish his doubt," she said. "Help him to believe that I forgive him."

She did not add anything for herself because she knew what she believed. She loved Jimmy and she had hope. Hope was everything.

"I will never give up hope," she repeated three times.

Closing the Blessing Box and blowing out the candles, she turned to her little anchor of hope on the bedside table. On an impulse, she took it out of the frame. She removed the gold chain from around her neck and strung the anchor from it in place of the cross Jimmy had taken.

Now her hope was close to her heart.

When she had made coffee, she came back upstairs again. There was something she had to do. She went into the spare room where Jimmy had put the computer and logged on.

She opened up Jennifer's e-mail and without reading it again, went straight to Reply.

Jennifer,

No way was she going to put "Dear."

This letter to you has been a long time coming. I had your phone number and many times I started to dial it. You don't know me and I don't know you but I know of you and I just wanted to contact you.

I know that you must be a nice person, because I can't imagine that Jimmy would have been with somebody who wasn't. I'm sure you're beautiful. I can understand you falling in love with him. I fell in love with him myself and I am still in love with him. I have been in love with him my whole life. You have only been in love with him a very short time. I know what you thought, that you could make plans with him, that you had a lot in common, that you were soul mates. But do you know what a soul mate is? A soul mate is not just somebody that you need. The true meaning of soul mates is when two souls are joined together. Our souls—Jimmy's and mine—were joined a long time ago. I hope that one day you will meet somebody who is available. You met

Jimmy under false pretenses and he wasn't available. You thought he was and it's nobody's fault. I hope you can get on with your life and understand and respect that it is better if there is no contact. I know you asked Jimmy if you could call him. I don't want to put words into his mouth. Speak to him if you must. But I would feel comfortable if there was no more contact. It would be hard to remain friends with him under the circumstances.

I wish you the best. I understand from Jimmy that you collect angels. I do too and I hope they can bring you some peace in your life.

Nanci

P.S. If you want to contact me, you can.

She felt a release.

Now she felt able to reopen the journal.

James,
I wonder if you have arrived at the retreat. I prayed for you this morning. This whole thing has certainly been intense for both of us. I know it will be worth every tear we shed. I agree the "up" times were more than the

"down in the dump" times. I do remember all those times you told me you couldn't sleep when you weren't in our bed with me. I hope you will get some sleep at the retreat. I will try and sleep while you are gone so as to be fresh for your return.

Life is short, like you were saying the other night, and how sad to throw love away because of a fear of the past. Today is what we make it, how we live it. I am willing to do the work to live in these moments . . . you are worth that to me.

Loving you,
Nan

She closed the journal and laid it on his pillow where it would rest beside her every night he was away.

She took a piece of paper and sucked the end of her pen. She needed to make a grocery list and go food shopping. Life goes on even when you are restoring your marriage, and they were out of everything. The list would be a long one.

But instead of Windex, butter, milk, potatoes, she put down these four words:

WHY I LOVE JIMMY

She continued writing as if she were being compelled to do so by another force.

He makes me laugh
He loves me as I am
He believes in the power of forgiveness
He makes me feel safe and loved
He leaves me notes and poems
He believes I can do anything
He's my hero
He remembers when . . .
He sings me love songs
When I'm sad, he's sad for me
He loves children
He's a big kid himself
He has taught me how to laugh at myself
When I think of Jimmy, I smile
And when Jimmy looks at me, I can feel his love

And she slipped the list inside the journal for him to find on his return, and went about her day.

Later that afternoon, Jennifer replied to her e-mail as Nanci had assumed she would.

Nanci,
Thank you for your e-mail. Believe me, I
thought that Jimmy and I were soul mates be-
cause we had so much in common. I under-
stand that you are not interested in hockey,
which I love . . .

It went on in a similar vein. Nanci was irri-
tated by the simplicity of the woman's letter.

Here was somebody who no doubt meant
well, but who obviously did not think very
deeply. But Nanci was always considerate of
other people's feelings, and she took care to be
patient in her reply to Jennifer, trying to make
her understand the situation. She remembered
Jimmy had told her that Jennifer had been with
abusive men in the past. When Jimmy came
into her life, he must have seemed like a hero
come to rescue her. It was ironic, Nanci
thought, that while she was working in a shelter with abused women, her husband was seeing another one far away.

Jennifer,
Sometimes in a long marriage people forget
that they were once friends, and the very
things that brought them together can drive

them apart. Jimmy and I had a lot in common, but because we were angry at each other, we forgot and we stopped doing those things to-gether. Yes, you can meet somebody new and discover "Oh, I like hockey, you like hockey, I chew gum, you chew gum. Boom! We're meant to be together." But it doesn't work like that and I hope you will discover one day that there is so much more.

Jimmy is a really nice guy. I know that. I forgot it for a while and in a way you helped me remember. I am sorry it didn't work out the way you wanted.

Nanci

Jennifer came back asking if Nanci would pick up the phone and call her. But Nanci said, *No, let's leave it like this.*

On Sunday, Jimmy called her from the Long Island Expressway.

"I'm on my way home. Meet me at the beach at five o'clock. Meet me at Promised Land."

Nanci took the back roads along the curve of the bay, past the osprey nest and the windswept pines. She turned off Cranberry Hole Road, driving past the little cottage she had rented during the Summer of Love. As she approached the water at the end of the road, she saw that Jimmy was already there.

She drew up alongside him. Together they got out of their respective vehicles, met up, linked hands, and silently made their way down to the shoreline.

Jimmy's face was grave. Not frighteningly so, just as if he were thinking seriously about something.

Nanci didn't say a word. She'd let him talk when he was ready. It was funny but she hadn't missed him while he had been away. She had been thinking about him so much, it was as if he had been right there with her.

He looked rested. And to see him looking so serious and thoughtful was a beautiful sight. He was so handsome. He did not seem to have aged from the time they had first made love here at Promised Land. She'd heard that when two people were in love, they never saw the other aging. Well, it was true.

She knew where he was taking her. The tide was out and the rusty remains of the ship's locker were still there.

"So," Jimmy said, turning to face her, "want to go skinny-dipping like we used to?" In one swift motion he scooped her up in his arms and pretended he was going to throw her into the icy February water.

The playful Jimmy was back. He set her down and they stood face to face, smiling into each other's eyes.

"Nanci, I have something to say to you." He brought her hands up and clasped them to his chest. "The retreat was everything we hoped it would be. No phones, no TV, no traffic, nothing to distract me. It was good to be with the guys there."

"And you talked?" She laughed. She could imagine the scene. A circle of unhappy men awkwardly trying to express their feelings, while Jimmy chattered away.

"Sure I did."

"But then?"

"Then I spent time on my own. A lot of time. I went over everything and there was no one to distract me. Finally I had a moment of solitude and surrender. I worked it all out. I thought of all the love we've shared and I remembered the tears. I realized that we can't undo the bad times. They are as much a part of our life together as the good times. But I want to forget about the bad times, I want to store them in the far reaches of my brain. All I want to remember are the lessons they have taught me."

All this time, he had been staring out to sea as he spoke. Now he turned to her again and drew her down to kneel before him in the sand.

It's almost as if we're praying, Nanci thought. *It's beautiful.*

"Nanci, I ask you first to forgive me for all the hurts of the past," he said. "I ask you to be patient with me because I'm still learning and remedying all those years of neglect and distance. I'm still a little unsure. I have to ask you to tell me your thoughts because I can't guess them. But I know that I am going to trust you. I know that you are the one who has the strength and the determination to keep our love going forever."

Nanci squeezed his hand to let him know she was listening intently.

He leaned forward and kissed her softly on the forehead before continuing, "In a way, we are working backwards. We are slowly remembering all that we forgot. Everything we are doing is like beginning again, becoming friends like we used to be, making plans, living out our dreams, the lizards, your writing. We've even started dating again. . . . There is only one thing left to do."

His hands went to the back of her neck and she felt him unclasping her gold chain.

From his pocket he took a little jewelry box. When he opened it, she saw the cross she had given him and next to it a little gold heart, exactly like the one she had lost long ago.

He slipped the cross back on the chain beside the anchor and put it into his pocket.

"I'll put it back around your neck later. First I want to say something." He placed the heart in the palm of her hand.

"You already have a wedding ring. So with this little heart, I ask you to marry me again. I want to take care of you, through sickness and health, good times and bad, forever and ever. Nanci, I love you anew. Do you take me to be your husband anew?"

Anew. It was a beautiful old-fashioned word filled with the hope that she believed in so deeply.

"I do," she said softly, lifting her face to be kissed, "I do, anew."

Their kiss at that moment was one Nanci knew she would remember and relive over and over again for the rest of her life. It was as if, standing there on the edge of the water, oblivious to the cold wind howling around them, bathed in the pink glow of the sinking sun, they were bound together as one person. She could feel his love embracing her and his warmth enveloping her.

They made their way back along the beach. "There's something else we can do for the second time and know that it will be different. We can plan our dream wedding," said Nanci.

"Tell me," he said, "how will we make our dream come true?"

"Let's get married on the beach, like we always wanted to, way back when. We can have a Handfasting Ceremony by the ocean where we tie a knot joining bracelets we will each be wearing, uniting our love as eternal. My sister Joie can perform the ceremony, your brother Harry can take the pictures. Our closest friends and our relatives can join us and celebrate our new beginning."

They spent the rest of the day by the fire, planning their wedding. When they went to bed, Nanci lit candles all around the room to illuminate their lovemaking.

In the semidarkness, Jimmy replaced the gold chain around her neck with its three charms: the cross, the anchor, and the new heart. The he slowly undressed her so that the only thing she was wearing as she lay beside him was the chain. He kissed each charm before finding the place on her neck where he knew she was ticklish. As they began to make love, they were laughing, but the bond between them grew so intense and so sweet that they both knew there was no need for anything other than the sound of their mutual passion.

And afterwards, as always:

"It's never just sex—we always make love."

"I love you, James."

*W*hen she awoke in the morning, he had already left for work, but there, on his pillow, the journal lay open.

Nan,
As you lie sleeping beside me, I am thinking
of some of the things that came to me at the
retreat.

I know I'm going to be walking around all day today with a big smile on my face. It makes me so happy to know you are going to be my wife. I can't believe the changes in my-self . . . what I feel in my heart. I know in my heart and soul that I have never loved anyone else but you. I smiled when I wrote that. I can't stop smiling. You are lying here beside me. You almost woke up just now. I am only sorry for allowing us to separate, for momentarily forgetting the love we share and have always had.

I'm sorry for not recognizing how hard you worked both at home raising our sons, as well as giving yourself to the little children at the shelter. I didn't realize how lonely it was for you not having me there each day. I love Charlie Raebeck and I think back on all our sessions and I wish I knew then what I know now.

I want to live with you in the present and the forever. I like this journal. Once I was skeptical of writing in it. Now everything has changed and we are so blessed. I used to think: same job, same life, bills, etc., how can it ever be different? The answer is: Us!

If I ever backstep, please remind me and I'll

remind you too, to talk about it. I want more
walks with you, more quiet days at the beach
or in the woods.

Sure as the sun rises and sets, I love you
forever.

James

She was incredibly moved. And then she
saw there was a postscript.

P.S. See over . . .

She turned the page to read:

WHY I LOVE NANCI
She's my Monkey-Girl.
Go figure!

At first she did not really know how to react.
And then she remembered the first item on her
list of reasons why she loved him.
He makes me laugh.
And she laughed.

EPILOGUE

☙

*I*t was a warm September afternoon a couple of years later. Nanci was turning the house upside down. She was looking for the latest copy of *Redbook* magazine. She knew she had bought a copy, she had left it on the counter in the kitchen. Meg Ryan was on the cover and Jason had put a cup of hot coffee down on her face.

But it was nowhere to be found. She had been looking forward to putting her feet up with it on the back porch for half an hour before Jimmy came home from work. It was Friday night and they were due to go to karaoke as usual. She had planned to wash her hair and sit out on the porch to dry it in the late afternoon sun. She went out onto the porch to see if she had left it out there earlier in the day.

"Where's my magazine?" she asked Garth and Daisy, the potbellied pigs, as they came snuffling toward her.

"If you feed us, we'll tell you," they seemed to be saying.

She went indoors and washed her hair, getting rid of her frustration at not being able to find the magazine by ferociously massaging her scalp. Then she started to sing while the hot water pounded down on her, exercising her vocal chords in readiness for the long night ahead.

Tying her robe around her damp body, she went into the spare room that she had turned into her study. She had her own computer set up, and she was writing every day.

She had an idea: she would read the magazine online. Going to the site, she studied the home page, where a tiny picture caught her eye. It was of a man and a woman walking along a beach, their bare feet making imprints in the wet sand. Behind them, white-crested breakers rolled into shore.

It could have been her and Jimmy.

Then she saw the words.

The Greatest Love Story Never Told.

It was a competition. *Don't let YOUR great love story go untold*, it read.

Looking for love? So are we. We're looking for The Greatest Love Story Never Told—a tale that captures the heart and lifts the spirits, one that moves you to tears and haunts you long after the telling. It can be poignant or funny, inspiring or surprising, unrequited love, steadfast love, triumphant love. All we ask is that it be true.

She didn't even look to see what the prize was. She double-clicked immediately on *Submit entry* and began to type.

The first time I saw my husband I was on a bicycle. We were about nine years old. He lived around the corner in a house full of boys. I am one of three sisters. Four years later we met. This time he was on the bicycle. He turned around to look at me and I fell in love. Thirty years later, he's still looking at me and I'm still in love.

We have grown up together and been there for each other through it all. Married at nineteen, parents at twenty, and again at twenty-six, we have survived diapers and night school, teenagers twice, the passages of marriage, and midlife crisis.

We go on dates every week, our favorite is singing karaoke together. We sing each other love songs. It may sound sappy and too good to be true, but trust me, this love is not taken for granted.

She pressed *Send* and began to towel dry her hair.

There was a very good reason Nanci had not been able to find her copy of *Redbook*. Jimmy had picked it up by mistake with a bunch of papers and taken it to work in his briefcase. He spent the day stuck at his desk doing paperwork, log entries, ordering parts for the helicopters that had to be shipped from other parts of the country, doing budget predictions for the next fiscal year. All day he had yearned to be out flying over the Hudson River, dropping scuba divers into the water, rescuing someone in distress and ferrying them to the hospital.

Meg Ryan stared up at him from the cover of Nanci's magazine, which he had discovered in his briefcase. *The painful truths behind her split*, read the caption to her story. So Meg had had problems with her marriage too. . . . Maybe he could give her a bit of advice, tell her to go see Charlie Raebeck. He picked up the magazine and was flicking idly through it when he saw the words: *Don't let YOUR great love story go untold.*

It was a competition searching for "The Greatest Love Story Never Told." All they asked was that it be heartwarming and uplifting. And true. Well, he had just such a story. It wasn't particularly exciting or glamorous or exotic, but in a world where divorce was the norm, the story of two people who had stared it in the face and turned their back on it was sure to bring hope to others in the same boat. It could definitely be described as uplifting.

Jimmy wanted people to understand that divorce was the easy way out, but working through the problems in a marriage was the hard part. He wanted everyone to experience the joy of newfound love that he and Nanci had discovered. At work he had a new nickname, The Preacher. The guys in his unit couldn't get over the change in him. Here was Jimmy LaGarenne telling them that they had to learn to listen to their wives, that sometimes guys had a problem listening. *Here comes The Preacher!*

He clicked on *Submit entry* and began to write.

Our Love Story started in Brooklyn, in 1970, at the age of thirteen. I went steady with Nanci for two weeks. We "broke up" because she wouldn't kiss with her mouth open. Still friends, I asked her out again on New Year's Eve, 1973. We married at nineteen years old in 1977. I guess with bad planning, our first son was born after we were twenty. We now have two. For two kids, having children, starting out so young, we struggled to scratch out the American dream. Working days, school at night. Through the hardships we had each other. While friends around us divorced, we had each other. I guess time, work, and complacency took its toll. Two years ago we came within a signature of divorce. I guess when you hit bottom in a relationship, the only way to go is up. I remember

Nanci on our wedding day. The way I felt when she walked down the aisle. I believe everyone should go back to that day when things get bad. We decided to do the work to stay together and now, two years later, we are living the love we felt on our wedding day and more. Working on twenty-four years of marriage. Sharing our lives as a couple should in this short life. I am a detective pilot with the NYPD. Nanci is now writing a book. We share everything from flying to diving. Clamming to karaoke. A walk on the beach to a hike in the woods. Poems and plays to breeding lizards. Also, the most important, our love for each other. I guess the catchphrase "soul mates" is valid. When Nanci sings karaoke to me, it's like we're the only two people in the room. When we're together, it's just nice. Like a sunrise or a full moon.

Whether this is printed or not, as I write it, I realize how lucky I am. Love? I can only hope others experience what we have.

NANCI AND JIMMY'S READING LIST

One Day My Soul Just Opened Up: 40 Days and 40 Nights Towards Spiritual Strength and Personal Growth, by Iyanla Vanzant. Simon & Schuster, 1997.

The Hurried Child: Growing Up Too Fast Too Soon, by David Elkind. Perseus, 1989.

The Soul's Code: In Search of Character and Calling, by James Hillman. Warner, 1997.

Passages: Predictable Crises of Adult Life, by Gail Sheehy. Bantam Doubleday Dell, 1977.

Getting the Love You Want: A Guide for Couples, by Harville Hendrix. HarperPerennial, 1989.

Journey to the Heart: Daily Meditations on the Path to Freeing Your Soul, by Melody Beattie. Harper-Collins, 1996.

The Pilot's Wife, by Anita Shreve. Little, Brown, 1999.

The Awakening, by Kate Chopin. Bantam, 1981.

Real Moments, by Barbara DeAngelis. Dell, 1995.

The Seat of the Soul, by Gary Zukav. Simon & Schuster, 1999.

The Power of Now: A Guide to Spiritual Enlightenment, by Eckhart Tolle. New World Library, 1999.

The Second Miracle: Intimacy, Spirituality, and Conscious Relationships, by Richard Moss. Celestial Arts, 1995.

The Book of Five Rings, by Miyamoto Musashi. Translated by Thomas Cleary. Bantam Doubleday Dell, 1992.